UNTOUCHABLE

MM BEAR SHIFTER MPREG DARK ROMANCE

JT FADER

STEAMBATH PRESS

Published by Steambath Press

A Creekside Valley Dark Romance

Cover art by Leigh Jarrett

eBook Edition published: September 2025

ISBN: 978-1-998008-90-2

ASIN: B0FPRJ58DT

AUTHOR'S NOTES

This book is about bear shifters. Men will shift into bears and back again. This is also an **MPreg** story. The Omega bear shifter males in this story can become pregnant and give birth anally.

This story is a **dark** romance with a happy ending, but it delves into **heavy and challenging** themes. The protagonist, Rory, carries the scars of a childhood marked by **sexual abuse** that haunts both his waking life and his dreams. The trauma inflicted by his **father and uncle** surfaces in his nightmares, and some memories are described in unsettling detail—though not explicitly graphic. This abuse forms the emotional core of his journey toward healing.

If these themes might be triggering for you, please approach this book with caution.

CONTENTS

Chapter 1

RORY

For the first time in my young, horror-filled life, I felt some semblance of safety as the thick log walls, warmed to a honey color by a small light, embraced us. When we pulled up outside the cabin we'd rented sight unseen, I hadn't been sure we'd made the right decision.

We were city bears, having lived our entire lives in Metro City. This cabin was deep in the forest at the end of a long, rutted dirt road. We'd bounced our way up in the beater of a car we all chipped in on buying to get us to Creekside Valley. I'd be surprised if nothing rattled loose.

It had rained earlier in the day. The scent of its cleansing purity mixed with the damp and musty earth clung to the tiny hairs in my nostrils. We approached the cabin, mounted rickety steps, found the key, and wandered around inside, checking where the bedrooms were and what kind of kitchen we had to work with. The air I inhaled smelled like mountain freshness and trees.

Or so I assumed, as I had no experience with either.

We were truly in the wild, deep in the woods. My bear heart kicked up extra beats as I thought about wandering through the trees outside and feeling the earth beneath my paws.

"What do you both think?" Carter did a few turns in the living room, hobbling on his bad leg, taking in everything. "It came with all the bedding, kitchen stuff, and even a television."

Jesse shook his head. "How the hell are we going to afford cable for the thing?"

I nodded in agreement but said nothing. I rarely spoke unless asked a direct question. Or if I had to initiate the forming of words at work. Carter and Jesse were used to me.

"We'll get good jobs. You'll see. It's going to be different here. I can feel it." Always so positive, Carter typically resided in his own little world. It was safer for him there.

He lived a life filled with forgetting.

All three of us did.

As well as being bear shifters, it's one of the things that brought us together and cemented us like super glue. Our varied and sordid stories emerged over time while we huddled in the putrid alleys of Metro City, trying to survive by doing whatever we needed to do.

We'd hit the streets, becoming homeless as teenagers for a variety of life-altering reasons—two of us by choice, like me. Now, after knowing one another for years, we maintained an incredible level of camaraderie, despite our differing backgrounds.

And today, we were here among the trees in a real house. It seemed surreal to have finally arrived. It had started as one of Carter's hair-brained ideas. Make enough money to leave Metro City and go live in the forest. Escape a life where our inner bears were never allowed to roam free.

It had taken us three years to make the money needed to pursue the dream. A dream we sometimes thought would never happen. I'd gotten off easy. I had a job repairing bikes and skateboards. At the age of sixteen, my boss had plucked me off the streets and given me a job.

After a few months, I'd been able to afford a dingy basement apartment. My only possessions in it were a few items of clothing, some basic kitchen tools, and a used and stained mattress I'd found. I saved as much money as I could, keeping it in a thick envelope beneath my floorboards.

As for Carter and Jesse, they were accustomed to dropping onto their knees for money. I'd done the same when I first arrived in Metro City four years ago. It was easy work, and having a cock rammed down my throat was something I'd become conditioned to enduring.

Years of practice meant I could easily switch off my brain and become a sucking, moaning receptacle. As long as they didn't grab me or tell me I was a good boy, it had been tolerable.

Now, after years of staying away from prostituting myself, I'd never be able to do that kind of work again. I couldn't stand the slightest touch from anyone, never mind having a cock in my mouth. And sex was out of the question. I'd become more distressed by touch with each passing year. It was deep-rooted in my very essence. My skin crawled at the thought of being touched.

And the nightmares ....

For the bulk of my nineteen years, nightmares plagued me. Recalling hands all over me as a child jolted me from my sleep, drenched in sweat, screaming at them to stop—to please stop.

I had never told them to stop while it was happening. I'd never found the courage, and I knew my pleas would be ignored. I'd become their plaything, and I learned to behave like a good boy.

I dragged my hand through my hair, barring the memories, and turned toward the bedrooms. Carter and Jesse were giving me first pick. I knew which room I wanted.

I stepped into the bedroom furthest from the front door.

"You good, Rory?" Jesse stepped up beside me. Not too close. I nodded and hauled my black garbage bag filled with everything I owned into the bedroom.

He left me to it.

I dumped the entire mess on the bed and picked through it, separating out my clothes. There was a dresser against one wall. I stuffed the top drawer full, a sea of black. It was the only color I ever wore. It suited my incurable depressed mood and my longing to be invisible.

Sometimes, if you were quiet and still, and hid inside your clothing, people didn't notice you. I had practiced those skills throughout my entire childhood.

The bed already had bedding, so I took my ratty quilt and tossed it onto a chair in the corner of the room. I could deal with it later. What was left on the bed were keepsakes I'd found over the years in various dumpsters around the city. One was a chipped, ceramic dolphin designed to resemble its slick body leaping out of waves. Another was a small, carved wooden bear.

I set them on the rugged wooden sill, then stood staring out the four-paned window. Nothing but trees as far as I could see. The nearest neighbors were reportedly miles away.

One more item remained on the bed. A small teddy bear that had seen better days, thrown away because it had become overly loved. I picked it up and held it to my chest. I often cuddled it in bed while I tried to escape the sounds and sensations of what had been done to me at night.

Teddy accompanied me over to the door. I looked at the passage set. It wasn't the locking kind. I would need to get that figured out before I closed myself off in my room tonight.

I took a deep breath to ground myself and then headed to the kitchen, leaving Teddy behind. I opened one cupboard after another.

There was a wider selection of dishes, pots, and pans here than I'd ever seen. I grew up in abject poverty. We'd only had the necessities.

I wandered over to the sink and looked out the window above it. More trees. It felt like my heart dropped into my stomach for a second, a moment of panic. Not being surrounded by the protection of blocks and blocks of tall buildings made me feel a little uneasy, despite the warm hug the cabin was giving me. Had we done the right thing?

My bear said *yes*. It clawed hard at my insides, wanting out to explore the forest. After running away from home at fifteen, I hadn't shifted until I secured that tiny apartment at seventeen. It was easier to sleep when I was in bear form. I would often dream of berries and salmon.

As a bear, it was rare for me to dream about all the time I'd spent locked up after trying to protect myself. As a child, from the age of ten, shifting into my bear form was the only way they wouldn't touch me, and I was punished severely for trying to escape them.

The threat of pain eventually kept me compliant.

I'd also shifted in parks at night a few times with Carter and Jesse over the years. It was the most dangerous thing we'd ever done. More hazardous than going off with seedy Johns.

It would be risky to fend them off if they became abusive.

Word would get around.

Even in human form, we retained much of our bear strength. It was something we rarely used because it would give us away, but the other homeless learned to never fuck with us.

Sticking together was a benefit to us. Finding two bears in a world of humans and wolf shifters had been miraculous. We'd spent many hours huddled together in the rain before I moved into my apartment. When I did, Carter and Jesse practically lived at my place.

During the last year, as we approached the dollar value of money we needed, they'd started going on *dates* in addition to picking up odd jobs and blowjobs. Men liked to keep them overnight. Use them a few times before pitching them back on the street in the morning.

They'd stumble into my place early to have a shower and clean off the stench, then crash on my bed while I went to work. It was rare I'd find them still there when I returned home.

Jesse also had light fingers that netted us a profit. While I knew Jesse, he ended up in prison twice for theft. Once for a whole year. The next was a minor two-week sentence. The judge took pity on him the second time. Jessed convinced them he was trying to clean up his life. That he had changed his ways. That he was on methadone and staying away from drugs and alcohol.

Both were *sometimes* true. The following week in our new home was going to be rough for Jesse as he withdrew from heroin and fentanyl. We'd checked to make sure Creekside Pharmacy had the medication he needed. They weren't in the habit of carrying methadone, but they promised to bring it in for Jesse. Unlike wolves, bears were susceptible to addiction.

It had been the catalyst for Jesse's parents to kick him out. That and he'd told them he liked males. He'd been much younger than me. He was abandoned to the city when he was fourteen.

The reason for going through withdrawal: The wolf packs that ruled over Creekside were vigilant about keeping drugs out of their territory. No one was stupid enough to defy them.

Jesse would need to learn to live without them.

Carter limped into the kitchen and pulled open the fridge. "Lots of room in here." He rubbed his thigh as he yanked open the crisper drawers. Dampness always made his pain worse.

His shattered femur and pelvis had never fully recovered.

"Rock, paper—scissors for who has to go to the grocery store," Jesse said.

My brow dipped. I didn't want it to be me—yet. I'd already driven four hours from Metro City to Creekside. I needed a nap, not a trip into the small town we'd driven through.

I participated in the game until it was just Carter and me. He got scissors to my paper. I groaned but dug the car keys out of my pocket. "Wanted to go anyway."

Carter's eyebrows rose. "Yeah? Why didn't you say so?"

I shrugged. "Need a lock for my door."

"Not what I asked, but okay." Carter unzipped the front of his fanny pack, retrieved four crumpled ten-dollar bills, and handed them to me. "Will this be enough to cover a lock, too?"

I nodded my head. I sure hoped so. I had no idea how much a locking passage set would cost. I'd need to go to a hardware store first and then use what was left to buy food.

It had been decided that Carter would oversee the money until we secured jobs. He had a head for numbers, and Jesse and I knew he would ensure we stayed on budget.

Jesse rolled his shoulders. I knew he wanted to come to me and give me a pat on the back to show he appreciated me taking one for the team by heading into town.

He knew better than to touch me.

What felt like fingers crept up my spine. Flashes of my dad's hands on me almost made me run to the bathroom to vomit. A sweat broke out on my brow and upper lip. I must be feeling unsettled. That's when he usually invaded my awake mind. I reminded myself that I had escaped.

"You alright?" Jesse asked. "You've gone pale."

I closed my eyes and nodded. "I'm good." I looked from Carter to Jesse, then left the kitchen. I took in a lungful of fresh air as I stepped onto the front porch.

It was raining again. The patter of the droplets as they hit the roof and surrounding trees was new. It was a relaxing sound. Made you want to curl up with a blanket and a cup of hot tea.

Maybe once I get back.

I'd seen some black tea in one of the cupboards.

I leaned against the railing, dug around in my hoodie pocket, and retrieved a flattened pack of cigarettes. I lit one and regretted the sight of the smoke floating into the pristine air. Seemed a shame to sully it with nicotine. I smoked half, pinched the ember end, then tucked the butt away.

The car took two tries to start, then the bumpy road from the cabin back to the main road jostled me around with some violence. Not sure I wanted to drive it often.

I drove slowly down Main Street once I arrived in town. Beside the grocery store was a small hardware store. I pulled into a spot perpendicular to the street. There were very few cars.

I wondered if there was some holiday happening that I wasn't aware of.

A bell jingled as I opened the door to the hardware store, and a male wolf shifter peered intently at me from behind the front counter. I ignored him and rushed down one of the aisles. From floor to ceiling, the shelves were packed full of everything you might want in a home.

I took my time, perusing.

At the back of the store, I found what I was looking for. A rush of anxiety overtook me as I discovered there were different types of configurations. I hadn't thought to bring the old passage set with me. I decided to take a chance and picked the cheapest one that locked with a key.

As I walked back toward the front of the store, I flipped the package over and read the instructions. I stopped short and groaned. I didn't have the correct screwdriver.

I had seen some screwdrivers while wandering the aisles. I headed back there and picked one that matched the requirement listed on the package.

Everything came to almost thirty-two dollars. We'd be eating lean tonight. I knew Carter and Jesse wouldn't hassle me about it. It wouldn't be the first time we'd gone to bed hungry.

After passing some crumpled money to the male who sniffed the air and sneered at me, I escaped and dumped my purchases onto the passenger seat of our car and headed for *Food Mart*.

It was only slightly larger than the store I'd just been in. Nothing like the food warehouses in Metro City. It was going to make shopping easier. I hated to be surrounded by masses of shoppers.

The air inside the store was cool. Outside, although it was raining, it was still warm. The summer was holding onto its August temperatures well into September.

I grabbed a basket and found the produce section. Three apples would be a start. And some late-season raspberries. I couldn't afford meat with the money I had left.

As I dug through the apples, looking for some that were bruised the way we liked, I sensed an Alpha bear approaching. His musk was strong and made my Omega body shiver.

He stepped up beside me, sniffing the air, and growled deep in his throat. I lowered my head and waited for him to speak to me. I squeezed my eyes shut as he came close to touching me.

"What brings you to Creekside?" His voice was smooth and sultry—and commanding.

"Moved here."

The Alpha snorted. "You rented the old cabin up Springs Road?"

"Yes." I knew better than to nod when an Alpha was speaking to me.

"What's your trade?"

I swallowed. I wouldn't call it a trade exactly, but it was the only thing I knew how to do other than suck dick. "Repairing bicycles and skateboards."

"You won't find many skateboards here."

I opened my eyes and looked at the apple in my hand. I picked two more and dropped them into my basket. "I'll find other work."

The Alpha grunted. I thought I was dismissed. I bowed slightly and went in search of the raspberries. My muscles tensed as he stepped up behind me.

I quickly placed a clamshell of raspberries with the apples.

"What's your name, Omega?" he asked.

Dammit.

I didn't want to engage any further. He should have lost interest in me by now. I wasn't in heat, and I didn't exude a friendly vibe. I chanced a look at him.

Holy fuck in a pickup truck.

I had to crane my neck to where he towered above the fruit and vegetables.

He was gorgeous. Prominent jaw covered in glorious dark stubble, and the most soulful brown eyes decorated with thick lashes. And his lips—so damned kissable, and I wasn't even sure I preferred males. I knew he was waiting for me to answer, but my gaze wandered.

Big and burly. Broad shoulders over muscular pecs that were barely contained by the tight chestnut t-shirt he was wearing. My bottom lip twitched as I returned my attention to his face.

"Rory."

The sexy Alpha extended his hand toward me. "Denver Rockland."

I looked at his hand, then back up into his eyes. "No." I usually didn't have to say more than that for people to get the hint that I didn't want to shake their hand.

Denver lowered his arm. "You afraid of germs?"

I shrugged. "Something like that."

He peered into my basket. "Is that all you're getting?"

"For now. Ate on the way into town," I lied. Truthfully, I was going to hit the dumpster behind the store once I left here. But he didn't need to know that.

Denver crossed his arms. "Are you *good* at fixing bikes?"

"My boss told me I am."

He tipped his head. "My niece has a bike I've been trying to fix … unsuccessfully. Do you think I could bring it to you at the cabin to look at?"

I swallowed. That meant I'd have to see Denver Rockland again. Even his name was sexy. My immediate thought was to say *no*. That I didn't have any tools, but that would be a second lie.

My boss allowed me to take what I might need to continue working if there were a market for it in Creekside Valley. He was always looking out for me and always trying to help me.

The human male had quite honestly saved my life.

"Whenever is good for you," I answered finally, then bustled away from him without the slightest bow in his direction. His continued presence had jumbled my nerves so much that I'd forgotten the protocol between Alphas and Omegas. He had received one bow from me already.

Maybe that was enough.

After I paid for the fruit, I went around behind the store and set my bag beside a dumpster. I could detect a delicacy I wanted to get my hands on. I clung to the front edge of the bin and swung my body up and into it. I found the garbage bag I was looking for and tore it open.

Inside were containers of cherry and cream cheese danishes. Likely stale, but we weren't fussy. I gathered some up and clambered back out onto the pavement.

"Rory? What the hell are you doing?"

I closed my eyes. Just my luck, Denver had parked out back of the store. I didn't turn to face him. I wasn't embarrassed to dumpster dive. It had kept me alive, but I hadn't wanted to be discovered by townsfolk so soon. It was so cliché, bears scavenging for food in the garbage.

I tugged my hood tighter around my face so I could hide within the folds.

"Was that fruit all you could afford?" he continued.

I nodded, then scurried over to my bag of fruit and added the danishes. I just wanted out of there. I didn't want to see the look of pity I knew would dominate Denver's expression.

I ran away from him as he called my name, leapt into our car, and nearly burned rubber as I left town. I suddenly felt exposed because he knew where I lived, as if his knowledge would somehow expose me to being found by my hideous family.

It was an unfounded fear. They would never look for me somewhere like Creekside if they were even looking for me. Maybe they'd written me off and moved on to a younger bear.

Fuck no.

I wouldn't wish that terror on anyone.

After nearly rattling my teeth loose on the road, I stopped outside the cabin. In the fading light, our new home looked cheerful and friendly; the warm lights glowed through the windows.

Beside the cabin, nearly hidden by the trees, was what looked to be a shed. I exited the car and pulled my tools out from the hatchback. The shed was a good place to put them.

I was surprised how spacious the shed was. I could work in there. There was plenty of room for a few bikes, and a workbench was located at the far end, where I could work on parts. It smelled of old oil and gasoline from the chainsaw sitting on the ground off to one side.

We'd need to learn to use both it and an axe if we wanted wood for the massive fireplace in the living room. I'd always wanted to experience a real wood fire. S'mores sounded amazing.

With the doors of the shed shut, I took the bag of food and my hardware into the cabin. I set the bag on the kitchen counter in front of Carter, then went to my room to work on securing it. I could hear Carter mumble, "Um ... okay," as he opened the bag.

I wrinkled my nose as I concentrated on removing the old passage set. Once I had it free of the door, I compared it to the new one in the package. Thankfully, they were a match.

After a few minutes of figuring it out, I tried out the lock, starting inside my room. Worked perfectly. Outside the door, I could use the key to lock and unlock it.

"Food is ready," Carter shouted. I pocketed the key and joined them in the dining room. Carter had cut up the apples, placing an entire apple on each of our plates, along with a pile of raspberries and two danishes each. There would be enough pastry left over for breakfast.

We were quiet as we ate, our bears invading our minds as we fulfilled our hunger. Even in this mode of my mind, I couldn't get Denver out of my thoughts: his husky voice and his climbable body. Him calling after me as if he cared. Even the scent of him lingered in my nostrils.

I cleared up the dishes after we finished eating, washing them carefully and placing them in the drying rack. I was exhausted. It was only 8 p.m., but I was ready for bed.

I made sure my door was securely locked, stripped down to my t-shirt and underwear, and climbed into the unfamiliar bed. The mattress was a lot softer than I was used to. The pillow plusher. I'd been using a folded wad of clothes to simulate one for years.

Everything smelled fresh and clean, like the sheets and blanket had just been laundered. Not the musty smell I was used to. Despite the differences, I soon fell asleep.

I was fast asleep. My eighth birthday party had been busy. In attendance were friends from both regular and bible school. My dad had gone all out with balloons and a real cake. Not the usual cake from a mix I was used to. I'd received so many presents, I'd been overwhelmed.

I remembered to take the time to open the cards, read them, and thank the giver before opening their present. Then announce what it was and thank the giver again.

Speaking so much was difficult for me, but I knew it was important. My dad had raised me to be kind and courteous. I came away from the party feeling good about myself.

The sound of my door opening startled me awake. I sensed movement, then the door was shut slightly, enough to leave a small stream of light across my bed and carpet.

I rolled over. It was my dad. I smiled at him in the darkness.

"Did you have a good birthday?"

"The best."

"You were a very good boy today." Daddy touched my arm. "I want to reward you."

I was suddenly giddy with excitement. The day had already been perfect. What more could he add to it? Daddy drew back my covers and nudged me to lie flat.

"You're going to enjoy this because Daddy loves you."

My eyes popped open, and I stared toward the ceiling. It hadn't ended there. Almost every night, my dad came to visit me. To reward me for being good. Telling me he loved me.

Then I turned nine.

I didn't want to go there, so I climbed out of bed, grabbed a pack of cigarettes, and stepped out onto the front porch. The first smoke was fast and frantic, clearing my mind. The second was leisurely as I grounded myself. I leaned my elbows on the railing and took in the complete blackness of the overcast night. The only light came from a lantern-shaped fixture beside the front door. I listened to all the cracks and creaks coming from within the forest.

Made you wonder what was out there.

I couldn't smell anything unusual, but then smoking cigarettes had dulled my sense of smell over the years. Carter and Jesse, after dinner, had spoken of shifting and going into the woods. Jesse had started feeling dope sick and was eager to find relief by shifting. Carter enjoyed a brief reprieve from his chronic pain, as his bear form allowed him to ignore it more easily.

Maybe that's what I needed. I stubbed out the ember on my cigarette and found the glass jar Carter told me he put on the porch for my butts, then stripped out of my clothes.

It was a thrill to be naked outdoors. Not strung up in my childhood backyard, but somewhere of my choosing. On my terms. I padded down the steps and into some tall grass, then got down on all fours and let my bear come out. A few agonizing moments later, and after recovering from the pain, I lumbered toward the treeline. I must have wandered for hours, finding the boundary of the cabin's property and where the wolves had claimed as their territory.

The world had never looked more alive. My eyesight keen; my ability to pick up faint scents and subtle noises, amplified. Being in my natural element soon changed my outlook.

I came back worn out but content.

Doors locked and tucked into bed, I clung to Teddy and thought of Denver. The image of him and the sound of his voice pulled me back under into sleep.

Not a single nightmare invaded my slumber.

Chapter 2

DENVER

I hadn't realized I'd nodded off until my best friend, Rick, knocked on my desk and woke me. My sleep last night had been broken and terrible. Thoughts of the young bear I'd met in Food Mart had invaded my usual deep sleep. I woke up in a panic at 3:12 a.m. for no apparent reason.

"What's up with you this morning?" Rick asked. "Not surprised I found you sleeping. You've had a glazed-over look in your eyes since you stumbled into the office."

I rubbed my hand across my eyes and around to the back of my neck. "Didn't sleep well."

Rick's eyebrows rose. "*You* didn't sleep well? That's a first."

"Yeah ... threw me for a loop." I checked my coffee cup. It was empty. "I had a vicious nightmare last night. Kept me from falling back to sleep for hours after I escaped it."

"A nightmare about what?"

I shut my eyes and shook my head. "Please, don't read too much into this."

Rick crossed his arms. "Now, I'm intrigued."

"I met a bear in Food Mart yesterday."

"Yeah?" Frank smiled at me.

I pointed at him. "See, that right there. Stop grinning at me."

"Okay ... okay, tell me about this bear."

"He's young."

"How young?"

I scowled at him. "I don't know. Maybe nineteen ... early 20s."

Frank flicked his hand at me. "Proceed. In great detail, if you don't mind."

My best friend professed to be only interested in females, but he always seemed to have a fascination with any of the males I had in my life. I indulged his curiosity.

I exhaled. "Exquisitely beautiful, dressed in black. He wore black boots, tattered jeans, and a hoodie with the hood up. He was tucked deep into it, as if he were afraid of the world."

"Maybe he is."

"That's the feeling I got off him. He stared at the floor a lot, and his knuckles were white from gripping his shopping basket so tightly. I was surprised he answered my questions."

"Omega?"

"Very much so. The scent of him from across the store nearly knocked me out." I rose from my seat, grabbed my coffee cup, and headed for the coffee machine.

"You were drawn to him."

I tipped some coffee into my cup. "I know what you're thinking."

Rick put his hands up when I turned to face him. "I'm not thinking anything. Tell me more about him, and then I want to get to the part where you had a nightmare."

"His name is Rory. He's renting the old Carter place."

"Those aren't the details I want."

I rolled my eyes, but let myself speak. "His lips are a deep crimson and look as soft as crushed velvet. When he speaks, they make the most seductive shapes."

To his credit, Rick didn't say anything.

"His eyes are dark and deeply haunted. Hidden behind thick lashes. Someone has hurt him. I could sense it deep in my bones. I had to fight an urge to gather him up in my arms."

"He triggered your DOM."

I nodded. "He was so shy and nervous around me. Bowed before I finished speaking to him."

Rick grunted.

"He barely had anything in his basket when he left me. I thought I scared him off." I sat behind my desk. "Went out back to get into my truck ...." I blinked and shook my head. "I found him digging around in the dumpster. He emerged with two packets of pastries."

Rick sank into a seat in front of my desk. "Did it feel like that's a regular thing for him?"

"He swung out of that dumpster like someone who's done it a thousand times before."

"Did you ask him about it?"

"No, he took off running. I called after him, but he ignored me."

"You didn't order him to stop?"

I clung to the handle of my cup. "I wanted it to be his choice."

"Can I back up a bit?"

"Go for it."

"Did he show any *interest* in you?"

I chuckled. "He certainly gave me a good look up and down. He seemed surprised when he first shifted his gaze from the floor to me. I think he liked what he saw."

"So, he might be a same-sex-loving bear."

"It's possible."

"And meeting him somehow invaded your dreams in a negative way?"

"It was the strangest thing, Rick." I knew I could tell him anything. I'd known Rick Turnbull since we were wild bear teenagers, rooting around in the northern forests of the state. We'd gone to college together. And set up our log home business as a team. He was there for me. "I felt as if *he* woke up, too—that he had a nightmare that ripped him from his sleep. That he woke me."

"You've formed an instant connection."

"It's the only explanation I can think of."

"But his age, sullen and shy personality, and the dumpster diving are giving you pause."

"I might be taking on too much if I approach him about our connection."

"Sounds like you'd need to ease your way into his life. If you decide to."

I took a sip of my coffee. I wrinkled my nose. I'd been so distracted, I'd forgotten to put creamer in it. "I'm going to be seeing him later today."

Again, Rick's eyebrows rose. "How so?"

"I'm bringing Breanna's bike to him. He told me that's his trade, fixing bikes and skateboards."

"So, you're going to use my daughter's bike to see him again."

"I've run into a dead end trying to fix it myself. Going to take it up to him."

"Guard yourself until you're sure you want to offer to take him on."

"That is a goal post that is way in the distance with this bear. He's not ready."

"You've got a good feel for him."

"He needs me to be gentle with him. I won't be going all Alpha bear on him."

"You know best."

Time to change the subject. "How are the logs that arrived this morning?"

"They're perfectly straight red cedars."

"Have the guys started spudding them?"

"As we speak. It's a big build, so it might take them a couple of weeks."

"That's the time I budgeted for. We should be able to make our deadline, no problem."

"It's going to be a beautiful home. Can't wait to see it come together."

"Which reminds me. I made a slight change to the blueprint in the powder room."

"Reconfigured it?"

"Yeah, I didn't like where the sink was."

"Agreed." Rick stood. "Good luck tonight with Rory."

I huffed out a laugh. "Thanks, I'm going to need it."

Rick left my office, and I was alone to run through my thoughts. Rory's clothes had concerned me ... I'm not sure why. It was a nagging feeling. Summer wasn't done with us. It was hot outside, but he'd been wearing long sleeves and jeans. Both had seen better days, nearly worn through in places. They'd barely made it through the laundry. There'd been a smell coming off Rory that was unpleasant. He was clean, but he smelled like cigarettes. I wrinkled my nose, remembering.

And yet, I was still tempted.

After work, I drove to my place and picked up Breanna's bicycle. Then I headed for Rory's. The cabin was situated at the end of a long dirt road.

It had been built many years ago. Turn of the last century. Mid-1900s. That's the thing about log homes. They lasted for at least three hundred years.

My crew had been involved in rewiring the cabin and updating the plumbing. It was a comfortable home. Had many cozy features—especially the river stone fireplace.

I pulled up outside the house. The door to the shed was open. I headed there with the bike. Rory spun away from the workbench where he'd been fussing and stared straight at me.

"You came," he said with a hitch in his voice, sounding confused.

"Told you I would."

He frowned and looked at the floor. "Didn't think you would after ...."

"After seeing you bolstering your meagre groceries?"

Rory nodded.

"Sometimes one needs to do what they need to survive," I said.

He peered up at me, then looked at the bicycle and pointed to it. "What's wrong with it?"

"I think the chain is fucked."

Rory smirked. "Technical term." He walked toward me and reached for the bike. He kept his distance as I passed it to him, then leaned it against the workbench and squatted beside it.

He fiddled with the chain. "The cogs on the cassette are completely worn down."

"Can it be fixed?"

"The chain needs to be replaced. Easy job with the right tools."

"Can you order a new one? I won't know what I'm looking for."

Rory rose and shook his head. "No credit card. I'll tell you what you need to order." He held out his hand. It took me a second to realize he wanted my phone. I unlocked it and handed it to him. His face screwed up as he scrolled back and forth, and back and forth, then sighed, relaxed his shoulders, and typed a few things in what I assumed would be my Notes app.

"I wrote down the website to order from, too." He passed my phone back to me.

"Thanks." I could feel creases forming on my forehead. Rory was sweating profusely, yet he continued to wear the hoodie. At least this time, he had the hood down. His hair was cut haphazardly as if it had been done at home by someone who had no idea what they were doing.

I inhaled the air. There were two more bears in the cabin: an Alpha and an Omega. I wondered if they were mated. Or if Rory was with the Alpha.

"Where did you move from?" I started.

"Metro City."

I waited for him to add more to his answer, but he didn't. "Did you live there long?"

Rory nodded, pulled a cigarette out of a package on the workbench, and lit it.

I immediately hated the smell. I'd been enjoying the scent of him. "I went to college there for business management," I replied as I stepped away from where the smoke was drifting.

He rolled his shoulders and shifted his weight onto one leg. He appeared to be searching for something to say back to me. He was in no way comfortable talking to me.

Hurt my heart a little.

He looked at me with his soulful eyes. "I'm sorry. I don't talk much. It's not you." He bit his bottom lip, then released it. "I don't mind you asking me questions." He took a long draw off his cigarette, making the cherry glow brightly. He leaned against the workbench.

"Okay. What prompted the move from Metro City to Creekside?"

"We needed a change. Nowhere to let our bears out."

"The two with you ... are they friends?"

"For the past four years. Found one another."

I felt like there was more to the story of how they'd met. But I wasn't going to pressure him by prying too much. If he wanted to tell me, he would.

"Are they mated?"

Rory laughed gently. "More likely to kill each other."

"And the Alpha ... and you?"

This time, Rory chuckled. "God, no. Jesse is absolutely not my type."

I felt the tension drain from his body. He didn't have the tight core of someone ready to run. Even if he did run from me, I wouldn't order him to stop. That's not how I was with my subs. Or potential subs. Even when I gave a command, it was a suggestion—their choice.

Rory stubbed out his cigarette and lit another one. Maybe I *was* making him nervous. Or maybe he was a chain smoker. It would be a challenge to help him stop smoking.

I decided to push my luck. "What *is* your type?"

He stopped with the cigarette a fraction of an inch from his mouth. "Don't know." The filter end found its way between his gorgeous lips. The putrid smoke filled the shed.

"Do you mind if we talk outside?"

Rory looked at his cigarette, then at me. "Shit ... sorry. I wasn't thinking." He quickly stubbed it out. "The guys are so used to me smoking."

"I'm not a fan."

"I'll remember that next time I see you." He led the way out of the shed. He went back to staring at the ground even though he was facing me.

"Rory." And then I waited.

He peered up at me after a few seconds. "Sorry."

"Nothing to apologize for." I smiled at him. "Give me a second." I jogged over to my truck and retrieved a bag from the front passenger seat. I'd stopped at Food Mart on my way.

I held the bag open as I walked toward him. "I hope you don't mind. Picked up a few things for you. Consider it payment for fixing my niece's bicycle."

Rory chewed on his bottom lip. I could quickly become enamored with the habit. He looked so innocent and unsure. I would enjoy building up his confidence if given the opportunity.

But that would be up to him.

Of course, I needed to be sure it was what I wanted before speaking about it with Rory.

"Thank you," he said.

I extended the bag to Rory. He hesitated, so I dropped one handle free so he could grab the bag without touching me. It worried me what the story was behind his haphephobia.

Fear of touch.

I'd looked it up on the chance it was more than avoiding shaking hands.

Rory licked his lips as he perused the contents of the bag. Sweet potatoes, leeks, raspberries like the ones he'd bought, a whole trout, and a tray of cherry and cream cheese danishes.

Luckily, there was enough food for three.

Rory bowed to me before he headed up the stairs and into the cabin. It rushed through me how I would've preferred for him to run into my arms and bury his face against my chest.

I had a lot to think about.

Not feeling like cooking, I drove back into town and went to *Growlers*, the only full-service restaurant in town. Jonas, the owner, smiled at me as I slipped into a seat at the counter.

"Haven't seen you in here in a while," he said.

"Been on a kick of making my own meals."

Jonas tipped his head. "Not tonight?"

"Other things on my mind."

"Yes, Rick told me. A new bear in town."

"Bears."

Jonas leaned on the counter with his elbows. "Really? How many?"

"Three." I grinned at him. "And no jokes about Goldilocks and the three bears."

He straightened up and swished his hand at me. "Wouldn't dream of it." He slid a menu in front of me. A formality. He knew what I wanted. Jonas served a great bear platter.

It was only a few years ago that our bear species emerged from hiding. The wolves, despite their incredible sense of smell, had never clocked us. They had assumed we were human bear hunters. The news had broken that other shifters existed when Creekside's own Lucas Black's son, Mason, had solved a murder case in Metro City, exposing a falcon shifter.

Staying hidden hadn't made sense after that. The wolf packs in Creekside and Riverton were known for being accepting and fair. Rick and I had been longing for community, so we'd gone to Maddox Black, the leader of the East Creekside wolf pack, and revealed ourselves.

It had gone well. He'd been expecting some shifters to come to light in Creekside. Besides Rick and me, there had been a couple of eagle shifters and four cougars.

"I've met one already," I said.

"Yes, Rick told me that, too."

I shook my head. "He talks too much."

"I think it's cute that you're smitten."

"Uh-huh ... well, Rory would present a challenge."

"One I'm sure you're up for." Jonas patted my hand. "Bear platter?"

"Thanks."

When the food arrived, I dug in. Jonas had added some nuts and fat grubs to the off-the-menu item. He knew how to run a profitable business. I appreciated how he catered to us bears.

It was a lonely drive home on my own after eating my fill.

The young bear, Rory, had infiltrated my mind.

I thought I was going to get through the night without waking, but my pleasant dream about Rory smiling and laughing turned black. His face twisted in anguish, and he started screaming, begging someone to stop. My heart felt torn open when I was unable to reach him before he was sucked into a vortex. So much screeching darkness pulled him away from me.

Sitting straight up in bed, my heart thundered, and I was perspiring. What did it mean? Was I getting a glimpse into Rory's nightmare? How strong was our connection?

Could I soothe the terror he was enduring?

I tried to sleep but eventually got up and went out on my porch to gaze at the stars. The pull across the valley was strong. In my heart, I knew Rory was staring at the same night sky.

Chapter 3

RORY

I didn't know where else to start. We all needed work, and the town was too small to support a business specializing in bicycle and skateboard repair. The bright red neon sign outside the only restaurant in town was impossible to miss, and it had a distinctly family vibe.

The name Growlers told me it was probably wolf-owned.

A bell tinkled as I made my way inside. I was here before the lunch rush, and when much of the breakfast crowd had finished. I walked up to the counter and waited until someone noticed me.

"Can I help you?" A handsome late middle-aged male wandered toward me. I could smell wolf on him, but he seemed too delicate to be one. His stature and wolf scent confused me.

"I'm looking for the manager." I made sure to make eye contact.

"I'm the owner." He placed one hand on his hip and shifted his weight to it.

I cleared my throat. "I just moved here. I'm looking for work. Do you have an opening?"

He put his hands in his apron and leaned on the counter. "You're one of the new bears."

"I am."

He looked me up and down. I'd worn some of my less tattered clothes. Still black. But I was as neat as I could be, and Carter had given me a quick haircut this morning.

"Have you worked in a restaurant before?"

I shook my head, then remembered to speak. "No, I haven't, but I learn quickly."

"It can get pretty busy in here. How are you under stress?"

"I've had lots of experience remaining calm."

He wrinkled his nose. "Okay, I'll give you a shot. One busy lunch shift. Sink or swim."

I smiled at him. "Thank you. You won't regret it." Thankfully, the owner wasn't looking for a handshake. I'd crossed my arms during our conversation, signaling that touching was off limits.

He placed his hand on his chest. "I'm Jonas."

I nodded. "Name's Rory."

"Well, Rory, I'll see you back here at 10:30 tomorrow. You can help me set up for the lunch rush, and I'll teach you how to use the cash register and card machine."

"I'll be here." I backed away from the counter. "Thanks again."

"All right." Jonas adjusted his apron. "See you tomorrow."

I turned and left, practically jogging to our car. I couldn't wait to tell the guys I'd gotten the chance at a job if I proved myself. I wondered how they'd fared with their job search.

After visiting a clinic to obtain a prescription for Jesse and then a drugstore to pick up his methadone, Carter and Jesse had scoped out the local businesses by chatting with the wolf at the hardware store. Carter had done some electrical work with his uncle before he ran away from his life, heading for the streets. When he'd learned there was a highly rated electrician company in Creekside, he'd been excited to approach them. I'd be picking him up first.

I made my way up a gravel-covered driveway to what appeared to be a compound. I'd dropped Carter at the bottom of the steep hill an hour ago. There were at least ten houses on the same driveway. Mostly log homes. As I sat waiting for Carter to emerge from a house with *Black Electric* signage, I drew a crowd. Maybe they didn't see much traffic up here.

This was an enclave of wolves. I could tell that much. The smell of wet dog was pungent and filled the cab of our car through my open windows; the only air conditioning we had.

An elderly male approached, came right up to my car, and bent down to look at me. He was enormous. And despite his age, I knew he could take me while in human or bear form.

"You one of those new bears?"

I nodded.

"And my brother Jonas gave you a job?"

I swallowed. Word travelled fast. "Yes."

The wolf grunted. "He's too kind for his own good."

I wasn't sure what to say to that. I had benefited from Jonas' generosity. Seemed my new boss was a wolf after all. I was saved when Carter came hobbling down the stairs with a huge grin.

The large male wolf backed away.

Carter threw open the door of the car and dropped into his seat like a bouncing ball. He was super excited. His meeting with the owner of Black Electric must have gone well.

"They're starting me on an apprenticeship tomorrow. Two years. Apparently, the beginning pay isn't much, but it's more money than I've ever earned being a cum dumpster."

God, I hated that term.

I'd been called that too many times in my life.

"I'm starting at the restaurant Growler tomorrow," I blurted.

"That's awesome! Two down. Hopefully, Jesse is as lucky."

I found a place to turn around and drove back to the main road. Before long, we were back in town. I went to the far end of Main Street and pulled up outside *Creekside Motors*.

Jesse was in one of the bays talking to a male surrounded by motorcycles. Jesse loved motorbikes and often spoke of riding one someday. Perhaps he'd landed a job working on them.

He turned away, then looked over his shoulder and gave the male a wave. He was smiling when he slipped into the car. "So, that went well," he announced from the backseat. I looked over my shoulder at him. He was a bit twitchy, but so far, he was faring well with the withdrawal.

"Will you be working on motorbikes?" Carter asked.

"Not right away. They're starting me off in the store, but once a week, they'll let me help the wolf, Harlan, I was speaking with. He had an apprentice, but they left a few years ago. He says he's open to taking on someone again if they're a good fit with the rest of the business."

"Is he the owner?" Carter asked.

"No, the owners are two male Omega wolves, Tyler and Patrick. I met them for a few minutes. I think they might be mated. They finish each other's sentences and touch one another a lot."

I grunted.

Two Omegas?

"When do you start?" I let Carter continue to speak. I was all talked out.

"Tomorrow morning."

"That makes all of us! This is so exciting. We'll be able to afford cable, a phone, and all the food we want with what we'll be making. My wage alone will cover the rent and electricity."

I harrumphed in acknowledgment of Carter's exuberant words.

As the designated driver, since I was the only one brave enough to drive, I took us home to our little cabin in the woods. We all changed into more casual clothes and found each other on the porch. It was noon, so the sun was high, but the shade of the trees kept us cool.

"We should have picked up some beer to celebrate while we were in town," Carter said.

I looked at the car. I could drive back, but one more trip down and up that driveway might drive a final nail in the car's coffin. I couldn't chance it. With all of us starting work tomorrow, we'd need to walk. I estimated the walk would take thirty minutes for Jesse and me.

"Are you thinking about the car?" Carter asked.

I nodded.

"My new boss, Maddox, offered to pick me up and drop me off every day."

"That helps," Jesse responded. "Rory and I can use our feet. Town isn't too far."

I tipped my chin in agreement with Jesse.

"I'm ready for a nap." Carter stretched his arms over his head. "That was exhausting."

"Me too," Jesse replied and pushed away from the railing.

Jesse followed Carter back into the cabin, leaving me alone with my thoughts. One voice in my head was my dad's, saying I would never amount to anything. So far, he'd been right; the past few years had seen me barely surviving. Maybe my life would be different now.

I knocked a cigarette out of the packet and lit it.

Drawing in a deep breath of nicotine calmed me. I focused on what tomorrow would be like. I hadn't been in many restaurants in my life. I hoped I'd catch on and not panic.

I woke the next morning feeling rested. I'd started having my usual nightmares, but then Denver had stepped into one and led me away.

Showed me some incredible sights around Creekside, up to the mountain peaks, and deep into the forest to a gem of a lake.

I'd been entirely focused on him.

"Well, this is it," Carter started once we finished eating breakfast—the last of the food that Denver had brought me for working on his niece's bike. The part should arrive in a few days.

"Yup," Jesse agreed. "Start of a new life working at normal jobs."

On queue, a massive, rumbling pickup truck pulled up outside the cabin to collect Carter. Black Electric must be doing well because the truck was a beauty.

"See you guys later." Carter hobbled to the door, his limp not stopping him from practically levitating. It made me smile to see him so happy. There hadn't been much of that in our lives.

"Gonna be a challenge for him to do any crouching," Jesse said once Carter closed the door.

"He'll figure it out." If he had to sit or even lie down, Carter would make it work. His disability rarely stopped him, but the horror of how it happened sometimes did.

"I should get going," Jesse said. "Don't want to be late on my first day."

"I'll walk with you. I can sit and have a coffee at the restaurant." I looked at the floor—enough talking. I was going to be overstimulated enough by the time my shift was over.

"Okay, let's go."

I made sure my door and the front door were locked before we headed down our driveway. The walk was boring. And at times, it was dangerous as we walked along the main road into town. There wasn't much of a shoulder. We'd need to figure out our way into town through the woods.

Shouldn't be hard.

I came with Jesse to the drugstore for his methadone, then to Creekside Motors and perused the store. It was stocked with automotive essentials, such as oil and windshield washer fluid, along with a variety of snacks and drinks. Nothing caught my interest.

I left when a worker introduced themselves to Jesse and said they'd be training him. He was going to be fine. It was me I worried about. I took my time walking to Growlers.

The restaurant was filled to bursting, everyone munching on bacon, sausage, and eggs. I took the last seat at the counter and lifted a menu from the holder. I had no money, except for a few dollars for coffee, but I didn't want to look conspicuous. The menu served as cover.

"You come early to watch the chaos?"

I looked up at Jonas, who had a handful of dirty plates balanced on both arms. I wasn't sure I'd be able to do that. Maybe I'd taken on too much. I tried to smile. "Checking out stuff."

"Let me get rid of these and I'll grab you a coffee." And then he was off into the kitchen. A female emerged from where Jonas had gone, carrying plates of food. She looked very much like Jonas, which was strange. She didn't smell entirely wolf. She smelled ... part human?

But then I couldn't trust my nose. Every scent in Metro City was so pungent and putrid that it overpowered the scents of individuals. Maybe I just needed practice.

"Here's a coffee for you." Jonas set a large mug down in front of me, along with a ceramic bowl of little creamers, some sugar packets, and a spoon.

Sugar was a delicacy. I added four to the dark liquid, then filled the remaining room with cream. It was essential for survival to take in as many calories as possible.

"Can I get you an apple fritter as well?" Jonas asked.

I must have looked uncomfortable, because Jonas leaned closer to me and whispered, "Not going to charge you for it. I want you well-fed and ready for work. Employee perks."

I cleared my throat and nodded. "Thank you."

What he placed in front of me was nothing like what you'd find in the grocery store. This apple fritter was large and plump, covered in a thick layer of sugary glaze, and had obvious pieces of apple visible within.

I closed my eyes as I bit down. It was like a dream. I enjoyed every mouthful to the fullest, alternating with the milky but strong coffee. I'd never felt so decadent.

When I was finished, I picked up my discarded menu and read through it, trying to memorize each item and its ingredients. I was lucky. My memory was good. And the items on the menu were straightforward. Lunch mainly consisted of burgers, soups, and sandwiches.

The female I noticed earlier strode past the counter and back into the kitchen. I could make out banter and laughter coming from where she'd gone. I hoped the kitchen staff wouldn't expect me to be talkative to them. I frowned and concentrated on Jonas' blurb to new customers instead.

Except for regular customers, his approach was the same every time. Welcome them. Tell them his name. Ask them if they would like something to drink. Go and get it. Give them some time. Then ask them for their order. Simple enough.

A little bell would ding, and the kitchen would call. "Jonas, order up." There was a mention of table numbers, which I hoped Jonas would cover with me. After a few bites, approach the customer and ask if they are enjoying everything. When they were finished, bring them their bill.

The transaction, whether cash or using the payment machine, only took a second.

I shifted on my seat.

I could do this.

I kept my eye on the big clock on the wall until it was 10:30. I slid off my seat and made my way to the end of the counter. Jonas ushered me behind it and handed me an apron. It covered my hips and had two pockets. Inside was a pen and a pad of paper. I tied it tightly around my waist.

Jonas perused what I was wearing but didn't say anything. I'd pulled my cleanest outfit out of the drawer of my dresser. It *was* a bit wrinkled. I'd have to be more careful about storing my clothes. Carter knew how to fold his belongings. I'd ask him to show me.

"You ready?" Jonas asked.

I nodded, then caught myself and said, "Yes."

"Jane?" Jonas looked over his shoulder at the young female. "Can you handle the tables until Rory and I go over some things and I get him up to speed?"

"Sure thing, Dad." Jane smiled at me. "Welcome to Growlers, Rory."

I gave her a nod. "Thanks."

So, she *was* Jonas' daughter. I had so many questions. The scent of mainly human rolled off her now that I was standing closer to her. Maybe she was adopted.

"Okay, let's run through what's behind the counter first," Jonas said.

He spent the next forty minutes showing me everything until I felt sure I was going to forget the simplest of the tasks and details. A few times, he almost patted me on the back. I knew I looked ridiculous dodging his hand, but that would be a deal breaker if he insisted on touching me.

Without a single comment, Jonas adjusted his approach with me and kept his distance. His acceptance gave me a warm feeling. My boss in Metro City had extended the same courtesy to me.

"Do you want to grab a cigarette before you start?" Jonas asked me.

Of course, he'd noticed the smell on me. Even a human could detect the number of cigarettes I smoked. I nearly growled with thanks, but used my words instead. "I'll be quick."

"Make sure you wash your hands before you come back out front."

"For sure."

It felt strange standing in the alley, next to a dumpster that I wouldn't be pillaging. I relaxed and let myself breathe, inhaling a combination of nicotine and fresh air. It was a good combo.

The next three hours were a mixture of pure laser-focused adrenaline and moments of confusion. Still, all I had to do was look over my shoulder, and Jonas was there to guide me.

I was surprised when I saw Jonas back behind the counter and realized my anxiety had eased. I looked around at my tables. Everyone was happy. I was doing it all on my own.

While grabbing a stack of napkins, Jonas leaned against the counter beside me.

"You're doing great, Rory. You really hustled through lunch. Do you want to stay for a few more hours? It'll be quieter. You'll have time to perfect your service style."

A genuine smile danced on my lips. "Sure."

Jonas pointed across the restaurant behind me. "You've got your first bear, over there."

My heart skittered around in my chest, the image of Denver surging into my mind. I turned, and my chest deflated. Instead of Denver, another bulky bear was sitting in the booth.

"Got him," I murmured.

I crossed the room, taking my time. A few steps away, the bear snapped his attention away from his menu and onto me. His gaze wandered all over me.

"Welcome to Growlers," I started once I reached him. "I'm Rory. I'll be your server."

"You certainly are."

I frowned. "I'm sorry ...?"

"I can see why Denver is taken with you, bear cub. There aren't many beauties like you wandering around Creekside."

My chest tightened, and my face felt as if someone had lit it on fire. The compliment was unwarranted and unwanted. What had Denver told this bear to give him the impression he was taken with me? Who was this bear? I gripped the bottom of my apron and looked at the floor.

"Can I start you with a drink?"

"Hey, I'm sorry." He sounded sincere. "I didn't mean to embarrass you." When I didn't look up or answer him, he placed his drink order. "I'll have a Growler's Ale."

"Be right back with it." I spun and headed for the counter. My confidence felt close to leaving me as I poured the beer, nearly messing up the head on it.

"You all right?" Jonas asked.

"Who is that?" I set the pint glass on the rubber mat.

"Rick Turnbull. He and another bear in town own a log home construction company."

"Denver Rockwell?"

Jonas' eyebrows rose. "You're the bear Denver met."

I frowned. Denver had spoken to Jonas about me. And he had talked to Rick, hopefully not including how he saw me lifting cherry and cream cheese danishes from the trash. Now that we were all making money from work, I was going to try to avoid shopping in back alleys.

Jonas laughed. "It's a small town."

"That bear, Rick, mentioned Denver." I lifted the pint onto my tray. "Threw me off."

Jonas tapped his lips with his finger. "Hm."

I furrowed my brow. "Hm, what?"

He fluttered his hand in the air. "Nothing. Rick will want a bear platter. You might as well put the order in for it before you head back over there."

I set the tray down, wrote the order along with the table number on one of my order chits, and set it on the passageway into the kitchen. Jonas had gone off chatting with customers.

Rick looked up as I set the beer in front of him.

"I put in an order for a bear platter for you. Jonas said it's what you'd want."

"It is." He turned in his seat slightly. "I really didn't mean to make you feel uncomfortable."

"It's fine." I looked down at my tray.

"No, it's not. Denver would tan my hide if he knew I embarrassed you."

"I'm not going to tell him."

Rick chuckled. "Yeah, but I probably will. We don't keep many secrets."

I didn't answer. I was too busy trying to control my breathing. Here was a bear who knew Denver well. Denver, who had helped me through the night. I didn't want to appear anxious to learn more about the comforting bear. My core tightened, making it even harder to breathe.

I wanted to know *so* much more.

"I have other tables." I made my escape before I humiliated myself further.

Thankfully, when I dropped Rick's bear platter at his table, the only words he spoke to me were *thank you*. And he left me a healthy tip. I was a little stunned when Jonas gave me a wad of cash from my share of the tips when I finished work and told me I had the job.

I hit Food Mart for food and beer before heading home.

This time, I trekked through the woods.

We ate well, celebrated, and decided on an early night. I was working the breakfast shift in the morning. The guys were both starting at 8 a.m.

After a cigarette, I locked up and crawled beneath my blankets. The excitement of the day filled my mind, leaving me even more exhausted. Didn't take long to fall asleep.

I pulled the blankets over my head. Today was my ninth birthday. My dad told me I would be receiving a special present tonight. My bedroom door opened, and I shut my eyes.

"Are you asleep?" My dad tugged the blanket off my head.

"No," I whispered. I knew it was pointless to pretend to be asleep.

"Good boy, you don't want to miss your present. Your daddy loves you."

"Rory."

I turned away from my dad. It was Denver who spoke. He was holding out his hand to me. I reached for it and let him cling to me and pull me into his arms. Into safety and security.

It felt like what love was supposed to feel like.

I buried my face against his chest and wept.

CHAPTER 4

DENVER

I could've had the bicycle part shipped to Rory's address, but then I wouldn't have had an excuse to see him again. I would have phoned him first, but I'd heard through the town grapevine that he wasn't going to have a landline installed until the next day.

Not sure why he didn't buy a cell phone.

Pretty obvious, Denver.

I recalled the dumpster diving. I had no idea about Rory's history. How what might be a chronic lack of money played into the way he lived. I knew so little about him outside of my insights into his dreams. The past week of Rory's nightly anguish invaded my sleep. I did my best to lead him away from the pain. I felt sure he sensed me there. That my comforting was real, that what I was experiencing was his actual nightmares. Not a figment of my imagination.

Rick started using words like *fated* when I mentioned Rory and my dream walking. But fated was strictly a wolf thing. I'd never heard about it happening to bears before.

Fated or not, something profound was happening between us.

My engine rumbled as I sat looking at the front of Rory's cabin. I shut off my truck and retrieved the bicycle part from my passenger seat. Beside the cabin, the shed was closed up.

The sun was setting. Maybe he was in for the night.

I clunked up the front steps and knocked on the door. The Omega bear who answered was plain-looking. Shaggy light brown hair. A scar down one cheek and through an eyebrow. And his lip was misshapen, as if he'd damaged it in an accident. He was short and thin for a bear.

He frowned at me. "Can I help you?"

"Is Rory here?"

The bear inhaled my scent and wrinkled his nose. "He's at work."

"Oh ... um." I should have known that. His scent was strong in the cabin, but not strong enough to indicate he was home. I held up the part. "He ordered this for the bicycle he's fixing for me. It's some kind of chain for it. It was delivered to my house. I've brought it here."

I almost rolled my eyes. I was talking too much.

There was movement behind the bear at the door. Now, this was an interesting looking Alpha bear approaching. He had old-fashioned mutton chops on his narrow and angular face.

"Rory didn't tell us about you," he said, his tone threatening.

The first bear shoved the mutton bear's shoulder. "I told you someone was out there with Rory last week." He grabbed the part out of my hands, turned, and limped into the dining room, where he set the part on the table. I guess he was done talking to me.

"Is that all?" the Alpha bear asked, his breath reeking of alcohol.

I didn't blame him for being short with me. They had no idea who I was. I mustn't have made enough of an impression on Rory to mention me. Or maybe he was the secretive type.

"Yeah, that's it. Tell him Denver stopped by with it."

"Denver. Got it." The door closed, and I was left standing on the porch. I plodded down the steps, wondering about the dynamics of three bears living together. It was unheard of in the circles I lived in. Bears were solitary. They even spent significant time away from their mates.

I dug in my pocket for my keys. I'd never had a mate. Not really. I'd had a few long-term subs over the years, but the relationships never progressed to where we were in love.

I wasn't even sure if I could love someone. Aside from my dad, the last person I'd loved was my mom, who had betrayed me. She'd run off when I was a young cub. She moved to France with her boyfriend, leaving my dad to raise me on his own. And he'd been amazing.

We'd been incredibly close.

Since my dad passed away two years ago, I felt alone in the world. I needed intimacy in my life. Kissing and cuddling time on the sofa. Spooned up in bed at night. Handholding.

I wanted it all in my life—a partner to be there for my some-times-needy self.

Maybe love would even find me.

When I arrived home, I felt unsettled. I couldn't get Rory off my mind. He was obviously damaged. Someone had hurt him. He would need careful guidance that was steady and safe.

I rubbed my hand across my face.

But was that me? Could I give Rory what he needed?

Should I even be entertaining this?

Plus, he was probably fifteen years younger than me. I'd never taken on a sub who wasn't close to my age. His inexperience with life would bring challenges.

I closed my eyes and tipped my head back, then rotated it to ease the tension in my neck. The dreams, though. The possibility that the connection we'd formed at night was real.

How could I ignore that?

The decision came from my heart, not my mind, and I went back out to my truck and headed into town. I sat outside Growlers for a few minutes. I needed to be sure.

I could see him through the window, rushing back and forth. The way he carried himself was heartbreaking. He had very little confidence. Occasionally, it would shine—then disappear.

I was doing this. I climbed out of my truck and went inside the restaurant. Rory didn't notice me as Jonas pointed to a vacant booth. I watched Rory, and I could see the instant he detected my scent. His spine straightened, and he inhaled deeply, then snapped his head around to look at me.

An actual smile danced on his lips.

He was breathtaking, even though he was wearing the same clothes I'd seen him in while digging around in the dumpster. I wasn't sure he'd found the laundromat in town yet. The scent of his clothes was ripe. Jonas was an angel, giving Rory a job opportunity.

I sat back and smiled at Rory as he approached my table. He was very official as he welcomed me to Growlers and asked if I'd like to start with a drink.

"What do you recommend?"

Rory fixed his gaze on the table, then remembered where he was and looked at me. My heart stuttered. I could swim a thousand miles in those deep, brown eyes.

My attraction was growing far beyond a sub situation.

"The Growler's Ale is quite popular."

"Then I'll have one of those. And ...." I looked at the menu. "A double cheeseburger."

"Not a bear platter?"

"I ate dinner a couple of hours ago. I'm not particularly hungry."

Rory frowned, and I could sense the gears grinding away inside his mind. He wanted to ask me what I was doing here, if I wasn't hungry. But he didn't want to be rude.

"I came here to see *you*."

I was going for the direct approach.

"Why?" Rory tucked his notepad and pen back in his apron.

"I needed to talk to you. And I think you need to talk to me, too."

Now, his eyebrows dipped, and he crunched up his nose. "I don't need anything from you."

I deserved that. Rory didn't know me, but I decided to take a chance. We weren't going to get anywhere until I learned a few more things about him. "Have I been showing up in your dreams?"

Rory's eyes widened, and he stepped back from the table.

I had my answer.

"I think we're connected somehow," I said. "Can we sit and talk about it after your shift?"

He stood there, staring at me, breath after breath, then his answer tumbled from his lips barely above a whisper. "I'll get your beer. I finish in fifteen."

For the next fifteen minutes, I watched a beautiful bear doing his best not to be noticed. He was attentive to his tables, but I could tell the interactions made him uncomfortable.

Jonas brought me my burger, but I wasn't hungry enough to eat it.

Once Rory took off his apron, his hood went up, and he shielded his face. Then he ducked into the kitchen. Probably going out back for a smoke before he came to sit with me.

Or, it was possible, he had absconded out the back door.

Five minutes later, Rory was sitting across from me, waiting patiently for me to proceed with why I was there for him. Why I had thought it was so important, I visited him at work.

"Can you tell me a bit about where you grew up?"

"Metro City."

"Were you born there?"

"Yes."

"Mom and dad?"

Rory blinked and looked down at the table. "Don't know what happened to my mom."

"So, your dad raised you?"

"My dad and my uncle." He swallowed hard after identifying them, like he was going to vomit. I could practically smell the bile. I decided not to dig any further into his family life.

"Did you like school?"

"When I went, I liked it. Didn't graduate, though."

Another thing to leave alone for now.

"My dad kept me from going," Rory continued unprompted. "He said school was wasted on me. That it wasn't for bears like me. That I wasn't good enough."

Fuck.

Seemed Rory had some stuff to unpack for me after all. I felt honored that he felt comfortable doing that. I kept quiet and let him speak. I didn't want to spook him by asking questions.

"First, it was public school, and then it was bible school. He took it all away. I lost all my friends. No one was on my side. I was so lonely ... but I got what I deserved."

Okay, that warranted a question. "What do you mean ... got what you deserved?"

Rory lifted his hands onto the table and played with his fingers. He stared at them as I detected a rise in his heart rate. "As I got older, I could be a nightmare. Not listening, fighting against him and my uncle. My dad was firm with me. I was grounded and punished a lot."

"And you think you deserved it?"

Rory's eyebrows furrowed, and he shook his head. "I don't want to talk about it anymore."

"Okay." I lay my hands on the table. "I was raised by a single dad, too."

That caught his interest. He looked up at me.

"My mom left when I was ten. Took off to Paris with her boyfriend."

Rory wrinkled his nose. "That sucks."

"So, we grew up quite similar."

Rory threw me a twisted and angry face, tinged by despair. "Trust me ... we did *not* grow up similar." There it was again—the pain. Same as when I pulled him out of his nightmares.

It was time to change the subject.

Chapter 5

RORY

I hadn't meant to spill to Denver. But he was there, and I felt at ease with him. More than at ease. He had rescued me many times in my nightmares. Led me away. Shown me incredible sights and held me as I broke down and cried. He was the one I turned to for comfort at night.

"After college, I signed up. I was in the Air Force for seven years," Denver said. I was glad he was the one doing the talking now. I'd revealed more than I ever wanted anyone aside from Carter and Jesse to know. Still, his presence felt like an island of safety and security.

I wanted to stay near that feeling.

"Afterward, my friend Rick and I started a log home construction company. It's been a fantastic experience seeing those homes go up seamlessly on site."

"I like our log cabin."

"Those fragrant, warm colored walls are like a hug, aren't they?"

I nodded. Every time I finished work, I couldn't wait to arrive home. To lock myself away in my bedroom and be on my own. The natural log walls helped me to decompress. It truly was home to me. So much moreso than the nasty basement suite in Metro City I used to rent.

"Can we talk about the dreams?" In slow motion, Denver reached forward, his fingers extended. He was going to place his hand on my arm. I jerked it away before he had a chance. He'd made me feel so unguarded that I hadn't crossed my arms. They'd been accessible to him.

My breathing quickened as I studied his face.

I'd hurt him by recoiling.

The distance was not what I wanted. Deep down, I yearned for the comfort he provided me at night. How would I ever overcome my abhorrence of being touched in my waking hours?

My dad and uncle had damaged me, maybe beyond repair. Every time I was touched, however gently, I was immediately sucked back to my childhood, their hands all over me, doing unspeakable things while I was screaming on the inside—the picture of obedience and submission on the outside, even faked enjoyment while they invaded spaces they had no right going.

I slapped my hand over my mouth. I felt sure I was going to be sick.

Denver nearly stood. "Are you all right?"

I took deep breaths through my nose, nodded my head, and released my mouth.

"We can talk another time, Rory."

I didn't answer, but after pulling my hood closer to my face, I slipped out of the booth and headed for the door. I knew he'd follow me. I waited as I lit a cigarette.

I wasn't sure what Denver wanted from me. His interest confused me. I was too broken to play with if that's all he was looking for. But then why all the questions? Maybe he felt sorry for me. Wanted to take me on as a project. I lifted my chin and exhaled a haze of smoke.

"Thanks for waiting for me," Denver said as he stepped up behind me, but kept his distance. "I wasn't sure you'd still be out here after I paid my bill."

"Needed a smoke before I head into the woods for home."

"And that's all?"

I grunted. He knew damned well why I had waited for him. Denver was right. We were connected. He was aware that he was in my dreams, interacting with me. It was some wolf shifter level shit. Maybe bears could be fated, too. Perhaps that's what was happening between us.

I tried to focus on my cigarette, but I desperately wanted to turn to him and fall into his arms. Kneel at his feet and wrap my arms around his legs and hold on for fear of ever being alone again.

Tears prickled the inner corners of my eyes.

I needed to get out of here. I tossed my cigarette onto the sidewalk and ground it out with my shoe. The mountain air was chilly without a coat, even with my bear furnace running. I wouldn't be surprised if it snowed in Creekside during the winter. That would be magical.

I'd never seen snow before.

"Gotta go," I muttered. "Long walk."

"I can give you a ride."

My core coiled into what felt like a knot. How could I be in his truck with him? I was on the verge of a meltdown. A walk through the woods is what I needed.

I nearly whimpered.

But I needed Denver more.

I stuffed my hands into my hoodie pockets. "Okay."

"Great." I knew if I looked, he'd be smiling. You could always tell if someone was smiling while they were speaking. I'd learned not to trust it.

Stop.

I furrowed my brow as I followed Denver to his truck. He wasn't like my dad and uncle. I knew his smile would be genuine. Not a ploy to try to put me at ease so I'd comply.

Once inside his truck's cab, I slammed the door and pulled my seatbelt into place. It was a newer truck. Nothing like the one Carter had been picked up in, but it growled the same.

I was thankful Denver was quiet during the ride. I was barely managing to keep myself together. One concerned word or question from him would be enough to make me split open.

We rumbled up the road to the cabin, the superior shocks on Denver's truck making the ride much smoother than it would have been in our car.

I felt a pang of sadness when we pulled up outside my home.

"It was nice talking to you tonight," Denver said.

"Um ... yeah." I fiddled with the zipper on my hoodie. I wasn't sure what to say to keep him here for a few moments longer. My potential breakdown felt soothed the longer I was with him.

"I see you there," I said. "In my dreams."

My heart pattered hard as I waited for him to answer.

"I try my best to lead you away from your anguish."

I nodded. "You do."

"I wish I could be there for you outside of your dreams as well."

There was the threat of tears again. I was delusional if I thought we could have that. I could never engage in anything meaningful with Denver. My disgusting history would make him run.

I swung the truck door open and bowed my head to him. "Thanks for the ride."

"Any ...." I slammed the door, cutting off what he was going to say, and jogged up the steps. I was inside with the door locked before Denver finished turning his truck around.

"Okay, who the hell is this Denver bear?"

I turned to face the living room. Jesse was standing in front of the sofa with his arms crossed tight to his chest, hands tucked into his armpits. He wouldn't be letting this go.

"I met him on the first day we moved here."

"Where?" Carter asked.

"Food Mart."

"And then the next day, he was up here." Jesse walked toward me. His eyebrows were pinched. He worried about me more than Carter did. Jesse saw everything that could go wrong.

"Dropped off his niece's bike for me to fix."

"He was here again today." Carter pointed at the dining room table. "Delivered some part."

"And now he drove you home?" I could hear the high-pitched concern in Jesse's voice.

"We sat and talked at the restaurant after I finished my shift." I didn't like to keep secrets from my two best friends. And this certainly wasn't the time to do it, even if I was in the habit. "And before you ask, I don't know what's going on. He's the one who seeks *me* out."

"He's certainly gorgeous," Jesse said.

Carter laughed. "Yeah, if you're into the rough and rugged type."

"It's not like that." I stroked the smooth carton of cigarettes in my pocket. "At least I don't think it's like that. He's difficult to read. I don't know what he wants from me."

"I think it's pretty obvious." Carter struggled off the sofa and went to the kitchen.

"Carter's right." Jesse exhaled heavily. "How does that make you feel?"

Heat rushed up my neck, prickling my skin.

Why would he ask me that?

I burst past him, toward the hallway to my bedroom. "You know exactly how that would make me feel. How can I be with someone if they can't touch me?"

Jesse jogged after me as I stormed to my sanctuary. "Rory, I'm sorry."

I couldn't turn around and let Jesse see me like this. Those tears that had been threatening were now spilling down my face. I wanted to hide. I wanted to hide and never be found.

I closed my bedroom door in Jesse's face and locked it.

Teddy was sitting on my bed, leaning against my pillow. I climbed on beside him and held him to my chest. I kissed the top of his furry, little, threadbare head.

He smelled musty and dusty.

He smelled like Teddy.

I closed my eyes and imagined Denver in bed next to me, his arms around me. I rolled over and pretended to put my head on his chest. My arm draped over his pecs. My leg tossed over his.

I imagined him kissing my forehead, then lifting my chin and kissing my lips. The beautiful picture came to a screeching halt when my dad barged his way in.

Stop it!

Please ... please, stop.

"Denver," I whispered as I dissolved into a whimpering mass.

His voice in my awake mind was unmistakable.

"I'm here, Rory. I'm here."

CHAPTER 6

DENVER

Last week had been the strangest experience of my life. Rory had been awake. I could sense it. His voice had come through as if he were standing beside me. When I told him I was there for him, I could feel his body relax as if I were holding him in my arms.

He hadn't called out for me again like that. I'd tried to speak to him in his mind a few times, but he hadn't answered. Not sure if I wasn't succeeding or if he was ignoring me.

We never spoke in his dreams—I didn't think it was possible.

Every night was the same. I found him in my sleep, restless and scared. Sometimes I had to pull him away from a mass of darkness, doing my best to distract and calm him.

Other times, he was waiting for me so he could rush into my arms to be held.

Our growing relationship was confusing.

I often went to Growlers so I could watch him. He'd found the laundromat. But his hair was still a mess. It felt strange exchanging simple pleasantries with someone I was beginning to hold a deep affinity for. Our sleeping relationship did *not* mirror our awake one in any way.

I looked at my computer screen. My attention had wandered so much that I couldn't remember where I'd been entering data on the spreadsheet. It was well past my usual working hours.

I recalled the last proper conversation I'd had with Rory, sitting in a booth after his shift finished last week. He'd sat so still, tucked into his hood as if he were afraid to move and be noticed. And when he'd yanked his arm away from me, like I was a live wire, it had hurt me.

We had enjoyed a breathtaking level of closeness in his dream the night before our conversation, which included him snuggling his face against my chest. Now, having him in my arms in my sleep most nights gave us both what we needed. Why didn't it spill over?

I lifted my phone from my desk and called Growlers. Jonas answered.

"Growlers. How can I help you?"

"Hey, it's Denver ... just wondering if Rory is working tonight."

"Why? Are you planning to do something?"

"Not really. I want to see him tonight to talk."

"He's not much of a talker." Jonas took a breath. "But then, you know that."

"He was open with me last week when we spoke."

"I'm glad. He's carrying around something dark. He does his best not to show it when dealing with customers, but it's clear how much it weighs on him. You can see it in his shoulders."

"Agreed. So ... is he working?"

"No, he has the night off."

I waited before I spoke. I knew Jonas had more to say.

"Be careful with him, Denver. I know that will be your intention, but try to temper your Alpha tendencies. I don't want him showing up damaged tomorrow morning."

"I won't push, I promise."

"Okay ... well, I'll leave you to it."

"Jonas ...?"

"Yeah?"

"Thanks for caring about him. He needs that in his life."

"Can't help it. My nurturing side comes out around him."

"You're a saint."

"Hardly ... now go talk to him. See you soon."

I ended the call and shut off my computer. I could deal with whatever I was working on in the morning. The pull to be near Rory was strong today. I knew he was thinking about me.

When I parked at his cabin, Rory poked his head out of the shed—over a week seemed long enough for him to fix Breanna's bike. It gave me a solid excuse to be here.

Rory ducked back into the interior of the shed as I approached.

Once inside, I could see Breanna's bike was off to the side. It looked like he had cleaned and polished it. My niece would be thrilled to get it back looking like this.

"Thanks for doing the bike."

"It was an easy fix."

"Do I owe you anything?"

Rory shook his head. "No, the food was payment enough."

"Then we'll call that settled." I danced my fingers on the seat of the bicycle, but didn't grab it. I didn't want to leave yet. We were being so impersonal with one another. We'd shared what bordered on intimacy in our dreams. The distant interaction between us now felt strange.

"Rory, can we talk?"

He almost reached for his hood to pull it up, but then seemed to change his mind. He crossed his arms instead and stared at the floor. "About what?"

"About what happens in our dreams. How close we are in them. How you rush into my arms almost every time. How you cling to me and cry almost every night."

Rory released a shuddering breath.

I walked closer to him and reached for his shoulder. He jerked it away and hurried to the other end of the shed from me. I could feel the tears well in my eyes. Who had done this to him?

"Please, don't try to touch me," Rory murmured. "I just ... I can't. I'm too messed up."

"Messed up how? Please talk to me."

He sniffed and wiped his face with the back of his hand. He was crying.

"I can't," he whispered.

I decided to accept where he was. I didn't want to put any pressure on him. Maybe someday, he would tell me. But then, perhaps he wouldn't, and our relationship wouldn't progress beyond what we had now. That possibility made my heart feel heavy and my soul sad.

"Let's go for a walk," I suggested. Being surrounded by trees always helped me when I was feeling unsure or stressed. Maybe calming Rory's inner bear would help him.

Rory moved toward the door without a word. I followed him around the side of the house and up a trail that was likely decades old. It was stripped clean of lower foliage from where the deer had been. And there were fresh and fragrant scratch marks on a few of the trees. Rory and his friends had been spending time as bears and marking their territory. I was comforted by that.

A tortured sound broke through the subtle quiet of the forest.

Jeezus.

He'd gone from crying to trying to catch his breath as he whimpered and sobbed. My chest tightened as Rory stopped, put his hand on a tree, and rested all his weight on it. The sound coming from him was beyond mournful. He was in so much emotional pain.

I wanted to help, but what could I do?

When he fell to his knees, still clutching the tree, my legs propelled me to him. I kept my distance but stood near enough for him to know I was there for him.

"Touch me," he whispered, barely audible above the breeze through the trees. He placed both hands on the ground near my feet. "Please, touch me."

I was hesitant, my heart thundering, but his desperation called to me. He was at his breaking point. Either I touched him, or it sounded as if he might lose his grip on his sanity.

I set my hand on top of his head, causing him to shiver. He moaned and relaxed as I pet his wildly shorn hair. His weeping turned to gasping for a solid breath.

Then his heart rate increased, and without a second for me to react, he shuffled closer, wrapped his arms around my legs, and buried his face against my thighs.

His body shook as he clung to me.

The ravens above were the only prominent sound besides Rory's heavy breathing.

He buried his face deeper.

"My life ... has been ... horrific," he said against my legs. I stroked my fingers through his hair and around the curl of his ear. His breath was hot, warming a small patch on my jeans.

I waited for him to speak, his sorrow causing actual pain in my chest.

"I'm so ... deeply damaged ... you wouldn't be here ... if you knew."

"I'm here with you now. Let's concentrate on that." He clung tighter to me as if he never wanted me to go. I would stay rooted here as long as he needed me.

"Rory, I'm here for you. Whatever you need."

He snuffled and pressed his forehead to my thighs, his grip wrenching the fabric of my jeans into his fists. His chest heaved with each breath he took.

He looked up at me.

"I mean it ... anything," I said.

Rory nodded, then buried his nose back between my thighs. I let him stay there as long as he needed. Something had shifted in him tonight to extend *any* level of trust to me.

He showed me similar trust in his dreams, but I needed to be cautious in our waking life. He wasn't in the same place as he was when asleep. I needed to keep the two separate for now.

When he rose to his feet, I tempered my urge to hug him. I'd let him lead the way when it came to touching him. Each step would be his to make. I'd never command him to do anything.

It's not what he needed.

He wasn't a sub ... he would never be a sub.

My feelings for him went far beyond that kind of arrangement.

"Shall I walk you home?" I asked.

Rory nodded and started ahead of me. I kept pace behind him on the narrow trail until it opened at the back of the cabin's property. He turned to face me.

"I feel embarrassed."

"No need. You had feelings that wanted out. I'm glad I was here to support you."

Rory's eyebrows furrowed. "Like in my dreams."

"I hope so."

Two tears ran down the center of Rory's cheeks. He wiped them away with the heels of his hands. "I need to go inside. The guys will wonder what happened to me."

"Will I see you again soon?"

"Give me some time." Rory bowed to me.

"As long as you need. Goodnight, Rory."

After I retrieved Breanna's bike from Rory's shed, the drive home seemed to take forever. I wanted to get back. To go to sleep. To see Rory again. To hold him after what had transpired tonight. But somehow, he kept me out.

Instead, I dreamed of him clinging to my legs, letting out small amounts of whatever pain he'd been enduring. Pain, that even in his sleep, he never let me know the source of.

Chapter 7

RORY

Two weeks passed since our walk in the woods. At first, I'd managed to keep Denver out of my dreams, but I'd eventually broken down and let him in. What we were cultivating there was special.

I knew I needed to decide if I was ready to be by his side when I was awake.

I finished dusting the living room. It was an ordeal. I loved the logs, but they collected dust, unlike straight walls. I moved on to the bathroom. It was my turn to clean it.

Carter had gotten it into his head that we had to transform ourselves completely. We no longer lived on the streets or in ratty apartments. Our home should be clean and welcoming.

He had a point. It did make me feel good to be surrounded by order. So much of my life had been without it. My dad had never been good about keeping our run-down house clean. It had almost been a hoarding situation. I had liked it at the time.

I could hide among the mess.

Over time, it rarely worked.

Even on a rare good day, I was lucky to be fed. Often, it was what was left over on my dad's plate, which he would place in a dish at his feet so I could lick it up. I never complained.

I was always a *good boy*.

I finished up and went outside, shifting to bear form so I could forget everything cleaning the cabin had brought up. Running through the woods, all my mind focused on was fresh air and the scent of wolves and deer nearby. And clear water. I headed to the creek for a drink.

I was out in the forest for hours, forgetting. The sun was low in the sky when I returned home. Carter and Jesse weren't back from work yet. I stared at the phone we'd had installed in the cabin.

The urge to phone Denver was strong. He had written his number on a piece of paper and left it with Jonas, with the words, "When you're ready."

I withdrew the worn paper from my jeans' pocket. I had looked at it and stroked his handwriting so often that the writing was fading. Now was the time.

I was ready.

I picked up the phone and dialed his number. He picked up after three rings.

"Rory?"

"Um ... yeah. How did you know?"

"Call display ... Jonas told me your number. You're in my contacts."

I wrinkled my nose. I had no idea how cell phones worked, having never had one.

"I was hoping you'd call today," he said.

My heart pattered a short, rapid rhythm. "I was thinking about you."

I knew instinctively that Denver wanted to bring up how close we'd become in our dreams. I wanted to discuss it as well. But not like this. Not with this much distance between us.

"Can I come over?" I asked.

"To my home?"

I straightened up. Had I overstepped? "Yes ... is that all right?"

"It's perfect. Do you need me to pick you up?"

"I'll find my way there." I wrote down Denver's address and directions and then waited for Carter to come home from work. Sometimes his boss, Maddox, would give me a ride into town for my night shift. I needed him to go a bit further this time, but I didn't think he'd mind.

When I heard his truck outside, I pulled on my hoodie and made my way out. "Just gotta ask him something," I said to Carter as he passed me and approached the cabin.

Maddox opened his window when I tapped on it.

"Hey, Rory, what's up?"

"I have a favor to ask. You can totally say *no* if it's too much of a hassle."

Maddox smiled at me. "Let's have it."

"I need a ride to Denver Rockland's house."

His eyebrows rose. "You and he have something going on?"

I looked down at the ground. "I'm not sure."

"Hop in. Not really any of my business anyway."

Carter was standing on the porch. He would've heard the entire interaction. I didn't need to add to it. I gave him a wave, then climbed into Maddox's truck.

"I have directions," I said once I was secure.

"No need. The thing about being the wolf pack leader, I know where everyone lives."

"Oh." I stuffed the directions in my pocket.

Once on the main road, we drove at least fifteen minutes in the opposite direction from town.

"Denver is an upstanding bear," Maddox said. "Never had any problems with him."

I nodded. Not sure if Maddox saw me do so, but he continued.

"You could do worse. By all accounts, he's a pushover despite his size. And he's very community-minded. He helps at the community center when he has a few minutes. Especially when it comes to the kids' programs. He's pretty wicked on the basketball court."

I hadn't known that.

But I wasn't in the mood to talk about it. I was concentrating on what I was going to say to Denver. *How much of my past am I going to reveal?* I wiped my sweaty hands on my jeans.

I would've missed the turn off if I had been driving. Denver's driveway was hidden, long, windy, and narrow—just enough room for a pickup truck.

It felt like we were driving deep into the woods.

When Maddox dropped me off outside Denver's house, I had to take a second. His home was gorgeous. And massive. Flared ends of ancient trees lined his grand front entry.

I felt insignificant as I knocked on his beautiful front door, adorned with a carved bear. The burly beast was fishing in a creek, a salmon between its teeth. I wondered if it was a self-portrait.

The door swung open, and I nearly walked into his arms.

I so desperately needed Denver to comfort me.

But I needed to talk to him first.

"Come in." Denver stepped back from the door, and I entered a foyer that opened onto a wide-open space with ceilings at least twenty feet high. The room beyond the foyer was arranged with leather sofas and chairs, and a stone fireplace that soared from the floor to the ceiling's top.

I was overwhelmed.

"It's a lot to take in for most people." Denver chuckled. "I may have overbuilt."

"It's your company. You can build what you want."

"True enough." He led me away from the front door. "Can I get you something to drink?"

"Do you have apple juice?" I had a penchant for the stuff since I'd tasted it at work.

"I do, actually. Love the stuff."

I followed Denver into the kitchen and leaned against the colossal island as he poured me a glass and set it in front of me. My hand trembled as I took a few swallows of the cold liquid, feeling incredibly nervous. I wasn't entirely sure what I hoped to achieve by being here.

I just knew I needed to be near him.

And open up to him.

"Should we sit in the living room?" Denver asked.

I nodded, left the kitchen, and set myself in an overstuffed chair facing where Denver had taken a seat on the sofa. I fiddled with my glass. Someone was going to have to talk first.

He beat me to it.

"I'm glad you called me," Denver started.

"I've been doing a lot of thinking, and I needed to see you."

I'd reached a decision. I would tell Denver something about my childhood. Some of my pain. Not everything. Not in detail, but something. If he ran, then so be it. It would hurt, but I needed to know now. Not in another two weeks. Now. Our dreams together ... I was falling for him.

Denver sat quietly.

I swallowed hard and stared at the glass in my hands. "I was physically abused as a child."

In my periphery, I could see Denver shift forward in his seat. I could sense his body tense, and he growled, low and rumbling, his Alpha male emerging. I knew in that moment that if Denver discovered who had abused me, he would hunt them down and kill them.

And it would be what they deserved.

For now, I wasn't ready to tell him any more of my story.

"By who?"

"That's not why I told you."

Denver grunted, and I looked up at him. His face was crimson, and his fists were clenched. It felt good to be important to someone in that way—someone on my side, ready to protect me.

"It's why I recoil when someone tries to touch me. Touching was never something to enjoy while I was growing up. I grew to fear it—even be repulsed by it."

The low growling coming from Denver became louder.

For once, it was he who needed comfort.

I set my glass down, rose from my seat, and sat beside him on the sofa. "It's in the past. I want to forget when I'm with you. Please."

Denver huffed, stopped growling, but didn't relax.

Fighting every adverse reaction in my body, I leaned against him, shoulder to shoulder. I gripped his arm and waited for him to calm down. His hand found mine, stroking my knuckles, and my inner bear, the basis of my soul, soared. This great big Alpha cared for me.

In the right way—not because he wanted something from me.

I shifted and set my head on his shoulder, still gripping his bicep, now with both hands. His fingers immediately carded my hair. I closed my eyes and allowed myself to enjoy it.

"The memories plague me," I whispered.

"The blackness in your nightmares."

"I can't get away from it. I only break free when you come for me."

"What was done to you?"

I shook my head. "Please ... don't. I don't want to talk about that."
I couldn't. We had a long way to go before I'd even consider telling
Denver what had happened to me.

If ever.

"Can I hold you?" he asked.

I bit my bottom lip. "Mm-hm."

Denver moved his arm until it was wrapped around my shoulders.
He hugged me to him, and I melted against his side. A wave of pure
warmth flowed through me that I'd never felt before.

Joy.

I felt joy and so much more. I tucked closer to him, smiled against
his pec, and hummed as he kissed the top of my head. My hand found
its place on his abs. His chest rose and fell.

That's the last thing my awake mind remembered.

The rest was in my dreamworld. Denver was with me. We were in
bear form, rambling through the forest and running and play-fighting,
thundering through the creek.

More joy.

Blissful, absolute joy.

Chapter 8

DENVER

Rory fell asleep in my arms as if he'd never slept properly before. His breathing was even and innocent, and I knew his mind was quiet—without nightmares. I took a chance and slowly lay down with him, my arms around him, layered against my body. He mumbled but didn't wake.

Lying with my back against the sofa, I tucked Rory's back to my chest. His head fit perfectly beneath my chin. I kissed his head as I inhaled the scent of him.

He'd become incredibly precious to me.

I closed my eyes and enjoyed our closeness. He'd taken a giant step today, initiating touch when he wasn't in the middle of a breakdown. He'd been completely level-headed.

I nuzzled the back of his neck and passed out, surrounded by the sounds of Rory's slumber. I'm not sure how long I slept for. Rory hadn't moved other than to jam his ass to my groin. We'd had a beautiful time together in our dreams. Running through the forest in bear form.

Not sure what woke me, but my mind turned to our conversation. *Physically abused.*

Who had done that to him? He was so gentle and soft spoken, why would someone come after him? He'd said his dad used to punish him. Is that who he was referring to?

My throat vibrated as I growled low, imagining his dad hitting him. If I ever encountered the cowardly bear who thought it was acceptable to beat his cub, I'd rip out his throat.

I felt Rory's body tense.

I restrained my growl. I hadn't meant to disturb his sleep. I kept still, but Rory started to squirm. He scratched at the front edge of the couch, then gripped it. I wasn't sure whether I should hold him tighter or wake him. Rory started whining, then yelled at someone to *stop*.

I knew he wasn't talking to me.

I tried to break into his nightmare, but the blackness pushed hard against me. Then I saw him, clawing to get away from someone. He was naked. I'd never seen him like that before.

And young. Rory couldn't have been more than twelve.

Large hands reached up his body to his shoulders and hauled him away from me.

A flash of what looked like rope followed him.

In my mind, I screamed his name, hoping to shake him loose.

Rory erupted in front of me, panicking and thrashing. I tried to hold him to me, but he struggled out of my arms and fell off the sofa, nearly smacking his head on the coffee table.

When he leapt to his feet and turned to face me, his eyes stared straight through me. He didn't see me. He only saw his attacker. He took off running, escaping through my front door.

I went after him. He shifted, so I did, too. It would be easier to follow him that way. As I sped through the trees, the distance between us grew wider; his youth outrunning me. I was at least four minutes behind him when I arrived at his cabin and shifted back to human form.

I hammered on the door. The wrong bear answered it. It was mutton chops. He surged forward, bumping his chest against mine, his Alpha bear going into full protection mode.

"What did you do to him?" he bellowed, then swayed on his feet. Again, the smell of alcohol was strong on him like he'd been bathing in it. I wrinkled my nose to block the scent.

"Nothing. I was holding him on the sofa. He fell asleep."

His nostrils flared. "You were *holding* him."

I knew what he was thinking. "He came to me. I didn't force him."

"I don't believe you. Rory doesn't do touching. You hurt him."

Please listen.

"I would never hurt Rory."

Mutton chops stepped back and crossed his arms. "He sped through that door traumatized."

I looked past his shoulder. The Omega bear was watching me from the living room. I brought my attention back to the bear blocking my entry. "Can I see him?"

"Absolutely not."

"You don't understand. Rory and I have a connection."

The bear from the living room limped to the front door and peered over the arm of the other bear, who had placed his hands on the door jam to keep me on the porch.

More alcohol. These two had been drinking heavily tonight.

"Rory doesn't form connections ... with anyone but us," the Omega bear said. "We're not going to let you hurt him more than you have already."

I growled and furrowed my brow. "I promise you, I didn't hurt Rory. He fell asleep with me. He had a nightmare. The same nightmare he has most every night."

The Alpha bear growled. "How do you know about his nightmares?"

"I often find him there and guide him away from the darkness."

"Impossible. You're not a wolf." Mutton chops gave me a good shove. "Leave." He wasn't nearly as big as me, but he was worked up enough to do some serious damage.

I took a reluctant step back. Rory was safe with his friends for tonight. I couldn't ask for more than that. He didn't need me. For all I knew, he didn't want to see me. My embrace had dragged him off to sleep. The feel of me touching him might have brought on the nightmare.

His friends were right. Maybe I had caused his horror.

"Let Rory know I was here."

The Alpha bear grunted and slammed the door in my face.

When I got home, the first thing I did was phone Rick. He had a way of helping me organize my thoughts. It was late, but he was a night owl. He'd be awake.

"What are you doing up?" he asked when he answered my call.

"Rory was over."

"Oh. How did that go?"

"Good at first. He shared a bit about his past with me, then came in for a cuddle. It was amazing, Rick. He felt like he belonged in my arms."

"But? I sense a *but*."

"But he fell asleep. Then woke up screaming and fighting to get away from me."

"A nightmare?"

"Yeah, a vicious one. I tried to get in, but it was so dark. I saw him for a second before two hands pulled him back into the black." I left it at that. Rory's abuse as a child wasn't my story to tell. "He fought me. He couldn't get away from me fast enough."

"Did you talk to him about it?"

"Couldn't. He took off, shifted, and ran home. When I arrived at his cabin, his roommates acted as gatekeepers. Wouldn't let me see him."

"They're used to protecting him. Do you blame them?"

I sighed. "No, I don't."

"But you feel like you know Rory on a deeper level than they do."

"In some respects, yes, but he's keeping so much from me. I wonder how much he's told his friends. If they know why he has these nightmares."

"They are three bears living together. They're either close, in which case, they know everything about him. Or they barely tolerate one another. I think it's the former."

I ran my hand through my hair. Rick was right. Bear one and bear two knew the reason for Rory's nightmares. They'd probably been watching out for him for years.

"What do I do?"

"I'm not sure what to tell you other than continue to be there for him. It seems like you can't help it when you're asleep. Are you able to speak to him there?"

"Only in my actions." I hadn't told Rick about when Rory had called for me while he was awake. It hadn't happened since. I wanted to keep it to myself for now.

"You're a kind and caring Alpha bear ... and it sounds like you have strong feelings for Rory. I think you should keep offering him what you have been and see where it takes you both."

"I hated to see him like that. It made my heart hurt."

"Um-hm. We're not talking about you being his DOM anymore, are we?"

"Not even on the cards."

"Never thought I'd see you so tied in knots over someone."

"Rory is special."

Rick chuckled. "I'm telling you ... fated mates."

I drew in a long breath, then released it. "You might be right."

"Denver, I've never heard of a bear being able to dream walk before. My bets on fated. And with that ... go to bed. Maybe you'll get a chance to see him again tonight."

"Thanks, as always, Rick."

We ended the call, and I had a cup of chamomile tea to help me sleep before I went to bed. I wanted to ensure I had the best chance of seeing Rory again tonight.

Chapter 9

RORY

I heard the front door slam and knew that Jesse had turned Denver away. Part of me wished Denver had fought harder to see me. The other part was glad to be alone. He would have looked at me with such concern in his eyes. I wasn't sure I could face that without breaking down.

I moved my arm from where it had been draped across my eyes and stared up at the ceiling. Light danced across it from the small, flickering lamp on my bedside table.

It brought back memories—my little bedroom with the peeling wallpaper, the only light from my barely open door. The first time my dad brought my uncle into my bedroom at night.

I remembered soaking my pillow with tears, sobbing.

I'd been ten.

Fuck.

I whipped my blanket aside, grabbed my pack of cigarettes, and headed for the front porch. I took a deep breath of the night air. I could smell remnants of Denver's scent.

I shook a cigarette free and then changed my mind, knowing Denver had been on my porch, looking for me after I'd shared some of my history. I didn't want to sully that with smoke.

He hadn't run.

I'd completely freaked out and torn off through the woods away from him.

And he hadn't run away.

He'd run toward.

I tapped the railing as my mind wandered—the nightmare I'd been having while in Denver's arms had been a familiar one. At thirteen, my dad and my uncle had started tying me up. In my room, in the basement, against the wall. Out in the garden, suspended from a tree branch.

Flogging and strapping my delicate skin.

At first, I'd been terrified—that's the part I'd been replaying.

My breath shuddered, and I dug my fingernails into the railing. It was about that time when my body started reacting favorably to what they were doing to me.

At least favorably in their eyes.

I'd been so confused; I started shifting to bear form when I heard them coming for me. The straps had really come out then. They'd whipped me and crammed me into a tiny dog kennel.

Every time.

Until I shifted back, and they'd release me, and ...

I tapped a cigarette out of the pack and lit it. Not sure why I smoked them. Maybe I felt like it was the only way I had control over the hot embers.

Denver.

I'd been so stupid to let him in.

Denver could *never* know. One look at my bare skin and I would have to explain to him what had caused the symmetrical scars that dotted my back, chest, and arms.

I needed to stop what was happening between us.

Love was something I would never have. I'd been resigned to that before Denver came along. And then he had made me *feel* things. He'd stripped away my carefully constructed fortress.

He'd invaded my dreams—given me hope.

I'd allowed him to hold me. That was something I didn't deserve. By the time I was fifteen, being passed around in men's sex clubs, I'd turned into someone I couldn't have imagined.

The night someone called me a nasty little cunt boy, every cell in my brain collided. I'd become what my dad and uncle had been grooming me to be. An obedient whore.

How could I ever let Denver know that about me?

Deviants didn't deserve love.

Denver would look at me with such horror and disgust that I'd never recover. I was already disgusted with myself. I didn't need to see it in Denver's eyes.

"Hey, Rory ...?" I recognized Carter's voice. "You all right?"

I nodded.

"Do you want to talk about it?" he pressed on.

I sighed. Carter loved me. He was only trying to help. "I told Denver stuff."

Carter hobbled up beside me and leaned on the railing. "How much?"

"That I was physically abused."

"That's only scraping the surface. Will you tell him the rest some-day?"

I shook my head. "I'm going to end it with him."

Carter was silent, then eventually spoke. "You let him hold you?"

I swear, I could still feel his arms around me. "I felt safe with him. He would never hurt me."

"You trust him?"

I stubbed out my cigarette. "Doesn't matter. He wouldn't want me if he knew the whole story."

"You don't know that. None of it was your fault."

I turned to face Carter. "Maybe when I was a kid, but I was complicit when I was older."

"You'd been groomed, Rory. It became normal to you to do what you were doing. You've told us that when you were being passed around at sex parties, you often sank into a fugue state. That doesn't sound like someone who wants to be there. It's why you ran away, remember?"

Not quite.

"In my head, I know that." I touched my chest. "But in here ... I'm not so sure."

"Because you sometimes enjoyed it?"

I nodded and lit another cigarette. The scent of Denver was gone now, obliterated by fragrant smoke. "I don't think I'll ever let anyone touch me like that again. Too many bad memories."

"It might be different with Denver."

I turned back to the railing and stared into the blackness. "Would it? No way to tell. Being naked in front of him would mean he'd see my scars. I'd have to tell him about how my dad and uncle used to put their cigarettes out on me. How I'd just taken the abuse."

"You were afraid of being beaten and tossed in that cage. Maybe it was the lesser of two evils."

"You sure know how to make a lot of excuses for me."

"They're not excuses. You *weren't* complicit. You were sexually abused, Rory."

"I know ... and I also know I would panic if Denver tried to be intimate with me. And that's the natural progression of a romantic relationship, isn't it?" I took a long draw off my cigarette.

"So, you're ending it."

I nodded. "Yeah."

"Can I weigh in?"

I sighed. There would be no stopping Carter even if I said *no*. I shrugged my shoulders.

"I think you might be making a mistake. You let him hold you. That's huge."

I so badly wanted to tell Carter how Denver walked in my dreams, rescued me, and held me while I wept. But if I did, he would put pressure on me to carry on with Denver.

"I'm tired," I said and left the railing. I ground out my cigarette on the lid of the jar Carter liked me to put my butts in. I dropped both cigarette butts into it.

"Before you go," Carter said. "Jesse is having a rough night. Started at work. He's been sweaty and nauseous. We're going to head into town tomorrow and get his methadone increased. If that's even the issue. I think he's been skipping doses, but he refuses to talk about it."

I groaned. I'd been so wrapped up in what was happening in my life, I hadn't been paying attention to what my friends might need. Jesse had a way of putting on a brave face.

"Do you want me to stay up with him?"

Carter shook his head. "No, I've got it. You work in the morning. Just wanted you to know."

"I feel bad."

"No, need, Rory. It's your turn next time he's like this."

"For sure."

Carter waved at me as he crossed the threshold into the cabin.

My sleep was restless, and I woke the next morning feeling like I'd been rolled over by a city bus. I finished two cups of coffee before I started my walk to work.

The breakfast rush was, as usual, insane. I was entirely focused on my tables until I detected Denver's scent. I ignored it for as long as I could, but damn, the pull was strong.

I slid a couple of order chits to the kitchen and turned to face the counter seating. Denver was sitting on one of the stools, nursing a coffee. Not sure what he expected to happen.

"I'm at work," I said to him.

"Yes, I know. I came here because your minders aren't here."

"They were running interference to protect me."

"From me?" His expression softened. "Surely, you don't think I could hurt you."

I exhaled heavily and crossed my arms. "How do you know I couldn't hurt *you*?"

"You wouldn't mean to if you did."

I shook my head—he didn't get it. I couldn't stop my history from hurting him.

"You're naïve."

His eyebrows rose. "Never been called that before."

"Believe me, I could tell you stories that would give *you* nightmares."

"Jeezus, Rory ... what did he do to you?"

Denver had figured out I was referring to my dad when it came to the abuse. I looked back and forth along the counter. The seats were full. "Not here."

"Out back? I'll meet you there."

"Okay." I needed a cigarette anyway. But I had told Denver I wouldn't smoke around him. I grumbled all the way to the back door in the kitchen. Outside, he rounded the corner of the building, and I nearly lost my determination to bring our relationship to an end.

He was beautiful inside and out.

No.

I couldn't cave. Our connection was so strong I would eventually tell him everything that happened to me as a kid. I couldn't do that to him. It would be too painful for both of us.

"I want you to leave me alone," I said as soon as he was beside me.

Denver tipped his head and frowned. "Why would you want that?"

"I'm too damaged to be in a relationship." Simple as that.

"Rory ...." He took a step closer to me. "I want to be there for you ... to work through it."

I looked at the ground. "There's no working through it. I'll be carrying this forever."

"Then I'll be there to carry some of it with you."

I raised my head and looked into his earnest brown eyes. He meant what he said.

I needed to scare him off.

"It wasn't my dad."

Denver straightened up and clenched his fists.

"It was my dad and my uncle ... and it was sexual." That's all he was getting from me.

Denver's face changed, partially shifting. His incisors descended, and he growled low and loud, shifting his weight from one foot to the other as though he was about to take off to find them.

To track them down and make them suffer for what they had done to me.

"I can't be intimate with you," I said. "I'm too traumatized by what they did to me."

"Then we wouldn't be intimate." I was surprised he could speak. His claws had come out, and his shirt was on the verge of ripping apart. "I'm happy just to hold you."

"That wouldn't be fair to you. You're a beautiful Alpha. You deserve to have cubs in your life."

"I don't want cubs if it means losing you. You're all I need."

"Denver, you're making this too hard. I want to end things. Please respect that."

"There's nothing I can say to change your mind?"

I shook my head and hitched my thumb over my shoulder. "I need to go back in." I turned after opening the door. "Stay out of my dreams. If you find yourself there, please leave."

His entire body appeared to collapse around his core.

I'd hurt him, but not as much as I would've if I'd told him my whole story.

I went back inside, my nicotine craving eating at me, but I didn't dare stay outside in case Denver took it as an opportunity to try to reason with me. I didn't trust my resolve.

I was distracted for the rest of my shift. I felt like crying, but I didn't have a single moment to dash into the office to release my feelings. Jonas must have sensed something was up because he cut me earlier than usual and told me to *go home and take care of myself.*

When I burst into the living room, Carter and Jesse were on the sofa watching television.

I dropped down beside them. "When did we get cable?"

"The installer just left," Carter answered. "Just trying to figure out the remote."

"He told us how to use it," Jesse added, "but it's not intuitive."

I couldn't help them there. Technology had advanced while we were living on the streets.

"I broke things off with Denver."

Carter switched off the television after hitting a few buttons. "How did that go?"

"I ramped things up ... told him my dad and uncle sexually abused me."

"Jeez, Rory," Carter said. "You just dropped that bombshell and then dumped him?"

"I gave him an out. Told him I could never be intimate with him."

"You don't know that for sure," Carter argued. "Sounds like he might be special."

Jesse grunted.

"Carter told me you let him hold you," he said. "What if you're in love with him already?"

I looked at my hands.

What if I did love him?

God.

Maybe I'd been hasty in my efforts to protect myself and him. I had made assumptions that he wouldn't be able to handle my past. That he couldn't come to love me through it all.

As I lay in bed, I fought the urge to reach out to him. Not sure why. Maybe I wanted to punish myself for running away from him. I didn't deserve him. I'd made the right decision.

I was better off alone.

CHAPTER 10

DENVER

Rick's was the last place I wanted to be tonight. But it was Breanna's tenth birthday, and I had promised I would be there for her party many weeks ago, long before I met Rory.

Long before he'd managed to rip my heart out.

September had given way to October, but the birthday kids wanted to play outside anyway. Rick and I were sitting on the back porch, keeping an eye on them, nursing a couple of beers.

"Do you think Breanna will shift soon?" I asked Rick.

"She's ten now, so she should be able to make it happen anytime. We've been preparing her for what the process entails and how to initiate the shift. She's been trying."

Rick's wife, Cynthia, opened the door and stepped out. "She's sure cute mid-shift."

I chuckled. "It'll be nice to take her into the woods when she goes full shift. See her reaction when all of her senses come online and she can drink in the beauty of being a bear."

Born as bear cubs, bear shifters remained in that form until they were four years old, allowing them to spend some years in human form before being able to shift back and forth at the age of ten. Breanna was right on schedule if she was partially shifting. I was proud of her.

"We'll have a celebration when she does." Cynthia pulled a chair closer to us, sat in it, and wrapped a blanket around her shoulders. She ran cold for a bear for some reason.

"Count me in." I took a long draw of the local IPA Rick had me trying.

"Rick tells me you met a bear."

"I did ... but I have no idea what's happening. It's complicated." I brushed the smooth surface of the beer can with my thumb. "He broke it off with me."

Rick sat up straight. "Why didn't you tell me?"

"I've been processing."

"Did he give you a reason why?" Cynthia asked.

I grunted. "He's afraid I'll run if he shares details of his past with me."

"That sounds ominous," Rick said, then furrowed his brow. "So, he decided to bail."

"Out of his life and out of his dreams." I swallowed. "That last part has been hard."

"Rick says you might be fated. Surely, that means you wouldn't judge him."

"I don't think he believes that. I'm trying to avoid imagining the details of what was so horrible, but I do know that whatever it is, I would be there for him—not run."

"Maybe he needs to hear that from you," Rick said.

"I told him. He ended what we were building anyway."

"Maybe you need to tell him again," said Cynthia.

I took a sip of my beer, then smiled as I watched the kids racing around the backyard in a game of chase that ended in tackling one another. You could tell Breanna was the only bear. She was vicious in her pursuit of her human friends. Maybe Rory had been right. I wanted cubs in my life. I took a long draw off my beer. *No.* If Rory couldn't give them to me, then I didn't want any.

My chest ached as my heart thundered.

I'd realized something last night as I lay there thinking about him.

I'd fallen in love with Rory.

It couldn't end like this. Not without us trying first. I left before the cake was served, after making my apologies to the family who had always been there for me.

They knew Rory was on my mind and that I was considering making a move.

I needed to be home.

As soon as I was there, I took a seat in one of my comfy chairs and called Rory's number. I had no idea if he was working or who would pick up the call and potentially keep me from him.

I relaxed when Rory's voice came through the phone.

"Hello?"

"Hey, Rory."

"Oh ... Denver, I thought I told you it was over."

"I decided I'm not accepting that without putting up a fight."

"I'm going to hang up."

"Wait, Rory ... please don't. Listen to me and really hear me this time. You can't scare me away. Whatever horrendous thing happened in your past, you can share with me ... or not share with me ... and I won't run. I don't want to run from you. Not for any reason."

Rory was silent.

"Please, Rory ... please don't shut me out. You don't have to tell me the details, but it's like I said before, I want to be there with you to help shoulder some of that weight."

"Sharing the weight would crush you. It's taken me a lifetime to learn to carry it."

"Then let me support you any way I can."

I could hear Rory swallow.

Was he going to listen to me or hang up?

CHAPTER 11

RORY

Denver was breathing heavily through the phone, waiting for me to answer him. My mind was torn as to what I wanted to do. I'd resigned myself again to being alone, but maybe Denver was telling the truth. Perhaps he would be as supportive as my friends had been when I told them what my dad and uncle had done to me. Revealing my past had brought *us* closer.

"Denver, you don't know the depth of what you're asking."

"Maybe not, Rory, but what I do know is I don't care if we're never intimate. I will always only go at your speed. If that means a lifetime of cuddles only, I'm okay with that."

"You don't understand. It's not just the intimacy and what I endured at their hands."

"Then what?"

He needed to know this. "It wasn't just my dad and uncle who did stuff. It was me, too. I was complicit when I got older." I dragged my hand through my hair. Or maybe I wasn't. Carter had reminded me that I used to zone out during sex parties ... but I often spilled my cum.

"Are you the same person now as you were then?"

I sucked in a breath, then rushed out a "No, not at all."

"And who do you think I'm falling for?"

Falling for?

I wet my lips, then shook my head. "But that doesn't make the rest of it go away. My experiences formed who I am today. I will never escape the wounds that have been left behind."

"Can I tell you something that shaped me?"

I wasn't expecting the change in direction, but I was glad of it. Hearing Denver's voice was bringing me peace. I could listen to him talk for hours.

"My dad and I were close while I was growing up," he started. "Even through college, I used to call him most nights. I came home every holiday to spend time with him."

I had a feeling this was about to take a dark turn.

"When Rick and I decided to come out as bears, we set up our company in Creekside. We'd heard the wolf pack here was open and accepting. We knew we'd have a good life here.

"I offered to build my dad a home in Creekside so he could be close. He turned me down. He wanted to stay in the house he and my mom had bought together.

"So, I used to go to visit him every month." Denver stopped, then cleared his throat. "I remember the day he phoned me and told me he had bladder cancer, like it was yesterday.

"I felt guilty that I'd left him behind. I should have been there for me. But instead of increasing my visits to see him, I froze. I was afraid to see him like that—sick."

Don't do this to yourself.

"Denver, that's a natural bear response."

"No excuse. I spend most of my life in human form. I should've been there for him. Instead, I was afraid to go home. To be there when he needed me most."

"I'm sure he didn't fault you."

"No, he didn't, and that made it worse. He told me he understood why I was staying away." Denver sniffed as if he might be crying. "Six weeks later, hospice phoned me."

"God, Denver ...."

"My dad, the man who raised me with such care, was in so much pain because the cancer spread to his pelvis, they gave him an incredible amount of pain medication, rendering him unconscious. No extraordinary measures. That meant he only had days to live."

My heart ached for the bear who had shown me such warmth.

I could feel his pain.

"It had been two weeks since I spoke to him ... I would never be able to again. He died three hours after I reached his bedside." He cleared his throat. "I learned something that day. I learned not to run away from situations that scare me. I should have been there for him."

"And that's why you say you won't run from me."

"It doesn't matter what you've done, Rory. I'll find a way to support you."

"Even though you might be scared."

"Yes, even though I might be scared by what you tell me."

I groaned. He'd broken down my resolve. "Okay ... but I need time to think."

"Take all the time you need. I'll be here waiting for you."

"I have to go. I work early tomorrow morning."

"Right ... okay ... goodnight, Rory."

"Night, Denver."

I hung up the phone and slid down the wall to sit on the floor. Was I prepared to tell Denver everything? Maybe not right away, but as our relationship unfolded.

Was I really doing this?

I struggled to get up and went to my room. The house was quiet tonight. Carter and Jesse were out at the only pub in town. They were checking to see if there were any humans available for a bit of playtime on a cold Friday night. I hoped they wouldn't bring them back here.

I hated listening to them having sex. At least here, they had their own rooms. They weren't rutting in the sitting room of my city apartment. Still, I needed complete peace to sleep tonight.

We had a large group of customers coming in for brunch tomorrow, and Jonas had given the table to me to serve. It was a great honor to be trusted with a party of fifteen or more.

I considered going outside for a cigarette, but decided against it.

I'd been doing that a lot recently.

I fell asleep replaying what Denver had told me. How not being there for his dad had changed him—that he was adamant about not running away ever again, even from me.

I closed my eyes and drifted off.

The room was dark, except for some red spotlights pointed at me. I gripped the leather straps, keeping my hands attached to the wooden, black X. My tears wouldn't stop. A response to my fear that seemed to be a turn-on for the many men in the dungeon, queuing up for my young flesh.

Please no.

I tossed the blankets onto the floor and leapt out of bed. I needed to forget. There was only one way to do that. I stepped outside into the cold air, stripped off my clothes, and envisioned myself in bear form until I felt my bones begin to move and reshape themselves.

During my shift, I thought about Denver and how he would react if I shared even half of what had happened in my young life. I concentrated on shifting, but his name was on my mind.

Not sure if I called out to him.

My brain certainly dwelt on him until I was fully shifted.

I ran into the woods, my claws digging into the soil. I kept going until I found what I was looking for. At the base of a fallen tree was a cavern that smelled of bear. The kind of bear that couldn't shift. It was an old scent, many months old. Too open to be a hibernation den.

I scooped some dirt from it to make enough room at the very back and crawled in. With my back against the rear wall, I curled up and let the innocent dreams of a bear soothe me.

Wind through the trees, gurgling creek, leaping salmon.

Denver's face appeared in my mind.

His bear face.

There was movement in the den. It woke me, and I growled, prepared to defend myself until I detected Denver's scent mixed with that of the bear crowding in against me.

I could have snarled and lunged at him to make him leave.

But he was hesitating—waiting.

It was my choice.

I grunted and rolled onto my back, relaxed. Denver took it as the sign I was sending and lay beside me. I lifted my head and nuzzled his snout with mine. He dug his shoulder into the soft soil and got comfortable next to me, his massive body blocking the entrance to the den.

I felt safe.

I snuggled up against him and closed my eyes.

It was the best sleep I'd ever had.

Chapter 12

DENVER

I was asleep on the sofa when I heard Rory call out to me. I tried to answer him, but all I got was a groaning sound and what I recognized as the snap and grind of bones shifting.

Rory was mid-shift, but he'd called my name. I wasn't sure what that meant. Was he in trouble? Had he had another nightmare? My heart raced, desperate to get to him, as I tore off in my truck, headed for his home after making a quick phone call.

It took me far too long to get to Rory's cabin. Once there, I found his clothes strewn around outside. I stripped out of mine, shifted, and followed his trail into the trees.

He'd dug in hard and took off running.

After over a mile, I snuffled around the soil where his scent was most potent. And then I saw it—a den beneath the roots of a fallen tree. He was in there. I plodded slowly toward it, allowing him to hear me, but I didn't sense him stirring. I found him asleep at the back of the den.

I grunted, and he opened his eyes.

His growl was throaty but unsure. He'd probably never fought another bear. I lowered my head and waited. If he wanted me out of there, he'd let me know.

Rory rolled onto his back and let his tense muscles relax. I moved in slowly, testing each step. When I was lying down, facing Rory, he nuzzled my snout with his.

If I'd been in human form, I would've been grinning.

Once I was comfortable, Rory snuggled closer. After grumbling in his efforts to practically become one with me, he settled down. His breathing soon evened out.

It was then that I was able to fall asleep again.

He stirred early the next morning, shoving at me with his snout.

He popped into my mind.

"Denver, I'm late for work."

"Well, hello there." Finally ... conversing in our awake minds.

"Denver, move." He shoved me hard with his paws.

"You're not late. Last night when you called out for me, I told Jonas you wouldn't be coming into work today. That we had things to sort out."

"What?"

"He was fine with it. He's on your side."

"You shouldn't have." He tried to roll over. *"I need to shift."*

"Rory ... you have the day off. Let's enjoy it instead of shifting and running."

"And do what?"

"Bear stuff."

It was light enough in the den that I could see him blinking at me in thought. We'd never been in bear form together while we were awake. In our dreams, as bears, we meshed beautifully.

Rory grunted and pushed against me with his snout to get me going. I angled my body out of the den and stepped into the morning light. Rory was close behind me.

We started by stretching and shaking our bodies to dislodge any clumps of dirt. Rory walked toward me and bumped me with his shoulder, then rubbed his cheek on mine.

He sniffed my snout, then slipped his tongue out and licked the corner of my mouth. I'm not sure if that was supposed to be a kiss, but I took it as one.

"What do you want to do first?" Rory asked.

"I'm hungry. Let's start there. I know where there's a patch of fall berries."

Rory nudged me.

I trudged along the ridge of the mountain until we reached what I was looking for. The berries hadn't been grazed yet, so Rory and I were able to eat our fill. After we were done, he took off running. I grunted and chased after him. Branches cracked beneath our feet as we thundered through the trees. Rory slowed down, and I was able to catch up to him.

I tackled him, and we rolled together. Playfighting was one of our favorite dream activities. Spending time with him like this awake felt so much more vibrant.

Rory roared and lunged at me. We both reared up, and he pretended to bite my shoulder but deliberately caught my hair instead. We tumbled down a slope.

This time, we didn't get up; instead, we took time to catch our breath. I growled and swatted him with my massive paw right on his snout. He sneezed and swatted me back.

"Salmon?" he suggested. *"Jesse says they're running."*

"I know just the place."

I lumbered to my feet and set off in the direction of my favorite fishing spot. It was a deep part of the creek, right at a ledge where the fish had to leap. They were easy pickings.

Rory splashed into the creek beside me, scaring some off. When a couple of fish leapt near him, he startled and backed away. Then approached the ledge and looked over it.

It occurred to me that he had never fished before.

I growled and huffed to get his attention. When he was looking at me, I stood poised and snagged the next salmon that jumped the ledge. Lesson over, I took it to the creek's bank, held it down with my paw, and ripped into it. In my periphery, I kept an eye on Rory.

It took him a few tries, but he finally snapped up a salmon and joined me to feast. We stayed there for hours. Fishing, eating, resting, and then repeating the cycle.

We wouldn't need to eat for a week.

I took us to a grassy clearing next. The fall sun was warm on the green blades. I shifted out of bear form and stretched out on the grass. Rory paced back and forth, hesitating.

"What's wrong?"

He grunted and huffed, shaking his head.

"Fuck, I'm sorry ... I didn't think." Of course, he wouldn't want to be naked in front of me. It might bring back terrible memories. I rolled onto all fours. "I'll shift back."

Rory growled and charged me, knocking me over.

I interpreted his display of force as an indication that he wanted me to remain as I was. I lay back and watched as he transformed into his human form. At first, I was mesmerized. Then I was horrified. I crawled toward him, wanting to run my hands over his skin.

What the fuck?

As well as a black tattoo on his left pec, perfectly circular scars covered his chest. And his arms. I whined until he looked at me. "Did you do this to yourself? Do you harm yourself?"

Rory shook his head and turned away from me. They were on his back as well. In places, he would have no way of reaching himself. Someone had done this to him.

"Did *they* do this?"

Rory faced me but looked down at the ground. "I don't want to talk here."

"Then where?"

"Let's go back to my cabin. Carter and Jesse won't be there."

Finally, names for Bear One and Bear Two. Now, who was who? I let that thought go when Rory reached out his hand to me and entangled his fingers with mine once I took it.

We strolled through the woods that way, hand in hand, enjoying the moment of being together as the forest surrounded us with sounds of the breeze, birds, and insects.

We were sharing moments I would never forget.

Rory was right. The cabin was empty when we got there. He collected his clothes from the front porch, yanked on his pants, and found the key to the door in the pocket of his hoodie.

I was surprised when he didn't insist on having a cigarette before going in.

Once we were inside, he pulled me along a hallway to a door and touched my chest to keep me from following him. He went into the room, then emerged with a pair of blue sweatpants.

"They're Jesse's." Rory pushed them at me. "He won't mind."

I grunted as I held them up, then somehow managed to pack my thick thighs into the fleece-lined pants. They naturally sat low on my hips. They'd probably never fit Jesse again.

My clothes were outside, but I'd been in such a hurry to get to Rory, I'd shifted while I was still in them, shredding them, creating a mess of useless material beside my truck.

After I had the sweatpants on, Rory led me to a door at the end of the hallway. He used his keys to open this door as well. It was his bedroom. I wasn't sure what we were doing there.

I wandered in behind him. It was a plain room: a bed, a dresser, a chair, and a bedside table. The only decoration was a pair of battered ornaments on his windowsill.

And a teddy bear on his bed. I sat on the edge of the mattress and lifted the threadbare stuffed toy from its place perched against Rory's pillow.

"Who's this?"

Rory smiled at me as he locked his door. "That's Teddy."

I chuckled. "Very creative."

Rory came over to me, took Teddy, and held him beneath his chin. My gaze wandered over Rory's body. He hadn't bothered to put on a shirt. He was muscular but lean with a soft belly.

His prominent hipbones protruded above the band of his pants.

Gorgeous.

I looked away and cleared my throat. "What are we doing here?"

He stepped closer and pushed on my shoulder. "Lie down."

I did what I was told and then waited. He took a few seconds before he climbed onto the bed with me and lay down facing away from me, Teddy clutched tight to his chest.

"Hold me."

"You're sure."

"I need your arms around me when I share with you."

I shuffled closer, careful not to press my dick against his crease, and threw my arm over him and pulled his upper back against my chest. He hummed and clung to Teddy and my arm.

I kissed the top of his head as I slipped my other arm beneath his neck. Once in a comfortable spot, he leaned back against me and played with the fingers of my hand.

"My dad first visited me on my eighth birthday. I was in bed after a wonderful day with my friends. He told me he had a surprise for me for being such a good boy."

I held my breath.

Jeezus.

"He did stuff to me that confused me. I wasn't sure how I was supposed to feel about it. It didn't feel like a surprise. Every night, my dad told me he loved me. I tried to like it."

I felt like screaming.

And vomiting.

I clung to him and blinked through the tears pooling and spilling from my eyes.

I swear, my heart was breaking.

"By the time I was ten, my dad had been taking naked pictures of me for a while. It turned out he'd been sharing them with my uncle. And my uncle wanted a piece of me for himself."

I sucked in a short breath. My urge to growl and roar was painful to contain.

Nothing like the pain Rory had endured.

"I used to shift to try to keep them away."

I put my forehead on the back of his head and breathed warm air onto his hair. I wasn't going to speak. Now was the time for listening.

"They didn't like that." He pulled my arm tighter to his chest. "They would beat me."

I couldn't help the growl that grew in my chest, rumbling between us.

Rory gripped my hand. "I love that sound from you."

Good thing because I didn't think I'd be able to switch it off. I nuzzled the back of his head and kissed it again. I breathed in the scent of him as it surrounded me.

"They would beat me and throw me in a tiny dog cage until I shifted back to human form. Then I'd be made to sit between them as they watched television and used me as an ashtray."

Fuck.

I wanted to hide him away. Never let him go. But it wasn't what he needed. He needed listening and caring me. Not protective and angry me. Not right now.

"Can I touch you?"

Rory tensed, held it for a few seconds, then relaxed. "Depends on where."

I rose on my elbow, and where he could see me, I kissed two of my fingers and then pressed them to one of his scars. "Just like this."

Rory groaned. "I like that."

I visited every scar on his arm, then rolled him forward and did his back. He grabbed my arm when I was done, lay on his back, and shoved me until I figured out what he wanted.

I straddled his hips and continued transferring kisses to every mark that marred the flesh of his chest. Even the skin around his nipples was scarred—white where they should be pink.

Rory didn't take his attention away from my face. Eyes wide, he watched me. I imagined he didn't dare close his eyes unless he imagined someone else in my place.

Rory set Teddy aside and placed his hand on my chest. He traced my collarbone to my shoulder and pulled on me. When I moved forward, Rory ran his hand around the back of my neck.

He was so close.

He dug his fingers into my hair, hauled me to him, and pressed my lips to his. His were soft and warm, and tasted of longing and loneliness. I was gentle with him as I kissed him.

Only a few moments passed before Rory placed his hand back on my chest. This time, asking me to stop. I reluctantly pulled away. I would always only move at his speed.

"Hold me again?" he whispered.

I climbed off him and returned to my original position. He pressed his back to my chest, hugged my arm, and kissed my thumb. He was exquisite in his tenderness.

"Now, you know more about me," he said.

"And I'm still not running."

He gripped my hand. "Are you disgusted with me ... for letting them do that to me?"

I lifted my head. "Rory, no. You were young. What they did to you was disgusting, evil, and cruel, but in your mind, they were the adults in the room. It's not your fault."

Rory inhaled, then sighed. "Thank you. I needed to hear you say that."

I lay my head back down and closed my eyes. I inhaled one lungful after another of his scent, my body warm against his, listening to him breathing.

I smiled when he started to snore.

And gritted my teeth when he jammed his ass back and flattened my dick against my balls. It took every ounce of concentration not to get hard. I wasn't sure how Rory would react.

I didn't want him running away in terror again.

But surely, he knew it might happen—that he'd accounted for my body's response to him.

After the shock of what he'd told me, the need for an escape into slumber prodded at the back of my eyelids. I tried to stay awake—I did. But I was pulled under.

Rory was facing me when I woke, his gaze fixed on my opening eyes. He smiled back at me when I grinned at him. He stroked my hair along my temple. "We passed out."

"Eating that much food will do that to you."

"A full stomach *and* brilliant company."

I chuckled. "So, I'm just company now, am I?"

"You know you're more than that."

Rory caught me off guard when he grabbed my face and pressed a quick kiss to my lips. It was short and incredibly sweet. He could pepper those on me for an eternity, and it wouldn't be enough. He licked his lips and used his thumb to rub my bottom one.

"I could get used to those," I said.

He tapped my chin. "I have more." Then smiled at me. "Maybe I'll share some again."

So beautiful.

My Rory.

A frantic rush started in my core, traveled up through my chest and neck, and caused my eyes to pool with tears. *Fuck.* How could someone so beautiful, who had endured so much, turn and be so open and cheerful and trusting when it came to me, after the hell he'd been through?

Rory wiped the tears from my skin when I blinked and set them loose.

"Don't, Denver. I'm all right. With you, I'm all right."

My throat felt dry as I tried to formulate what I wanted to say to him. His growing trust in me made me feel honored to be in his presence. "I'm in awe of you."

Rory stroked the curl of my ear, then raked his fingers into my hair. He closed his eyes and drew closer to me. This time, the kiss didn't end right away. It was deeper, and he draped his leg over mine and almost dragged every measure of restraint I had for him right out of me.

He cupped my jawline and clung to it as he devastated my lips, moaning and sighing. Out of respect and uncertainty, I kept my hands to myself and let him explore at his own pace. I smiled against his lips when he grabbed my hand and placed it on his hip. I clung to it ever so gently.

With our lips softly devouring, I was elevated to a place of complete serenity—and oneness with Rory. We were taking steps further than we had in our shared dreams.

The flow reaching its crest, Rory gasped as he relinquished my mouth and immediately darted his eyes away from my gaze. His confidence would come and go. I had anticipated that.

I stayed where I was, giving Rory space, as he leapt from the bed and paced the room from one end to the other. He dragged his hand through his hair, intermittently grasping handfuls.

He stopped, then unlocked and opened his bedroom door.

I sat up. "Do you want me to leave?"

He shook his head. "I want you to meet Carter and Jesse."

"Like this?" I swung my legs off the bed. "I'm not exactly ready for meeting folks." I'd tried to stop it, but my dick was in a half-chub situation from kissing Rory.

He chewed on his bottom lip as his gaze perused what I had no way of hiding. He seemed more appreciative than traumatized.

"You know, I wasn't sure I liked males," Rory said. "Or if it was just conditioning."

"And now?" I rose to my feet.

Rory stepped forward and brushed his fingers through the hair on my pecs. "It feels right with you." His fingers lingered, then he trailed them down my arm and gripped my hand. "Come on."

"Not even going to give me a second, hey?"

"You'll be fine."

As we approached the living room, I wondered what time it was. Shouldn't his friends be asleep? Instead, we found them sitting on the sofa with a bottle of vodka on the coffee table.

I frowned when the Alpha poured himself a full glass of straight spirits.

At least the Omega was mixing his with orange juice.

Rory clung to my arm. "Guys?"

There was no need to get their attention. They were already staring at me. The Alpha scowled as his scrutiny raked over me. It was evident by the fact I had no clothes other than his sweatpants that I had been naked. He rose to his feet. I could feel his inner hackles bristling.

"Your stench has permeated the cabin, Alpha," he said in a deep, guttural tone.

"Jesse, stop." Rory pulled me further into the room. "Denver isn't a rival." He pointed at the one he'd called Jesse. "That's Jesse, and over there is Carter."

I nodded. "Pleasure."

Jesse started a low growl that evolved into speech. "Where were you last night, Rory?"

Rory crossed his arms. "I shifted and spent the night in a den."

"And today? I thought you were working this morning."

"Denver and I went fishing. I took the day off." He sighed. "Are you finished?"

Jesse grunted.

"We thought about busting down your door when we got home," Carter said. "But you were quiet in there. Figured you must be sleeping." He smiled. "Or that Denver had killed you."

Rory clung tighter to my arm, holding it down the front of his body. "We were cuddling."

Jesse growled and took off toward the kitchen.

I frowned. "Honestly, what *is* his problem?"

"He's used to protecting Rory." Carter took a swallow of his drink and drained the glass. He also had the container of orange juice on the coffee table. His next pour was mostly vodka.

"The day we met, he rescued me from someone," Rory said.

Jesse returned to the living room. "That John had no business roughing you up."

My heart did a double-take.

John?

Rory had been a sex worker?

Jesse stared at me, challenging me.

"Jesse!" Rory released my arm. "How could you!" He backed away from me, covered his mouth, and looked at me with such a desperate pleading expression that my breath caught.

Rory hadn't wanted me to know this fact about him.

This was part of his history.

It had made him who he was today.

I wasn't going to judge him for it. He must've been in survival mode.

I walked toward him. "Rory ...." I held out my arms. Tears streamed down his cheeks as he ran into my embrace. I kissed his head as I squeezed him to me. "Still not running."

"I was always so hungry," Rory managed to get out amid his tears.

I pressed my nose to his head. "You don't need to explain it to me. I'm here for you." I looked up and glared at Jesse. How could he be so cruel to someone he supposedly cared for?

Jesse sloshed another abundant pour of vodka into his glass.

The clue might be right there.

"See me out?" I said to Rory. "It's late."

"Wish you could stay." He kept hold of my arm as we walked to the door.

"Not tonight, okay." We stepped onto the front porch, and Rory closed the door behind us. "I don't think your friends want me here. We can shift near my place next time."

"I'd like that." Rory looked at his hands, then back up at me, tears on his cheeks. He was waiting for me to say goodnight. Waiting for me to kiss him. I swept my hand into his hair.

"Goodnight, Rory."

His breath was hot on my lips as I descended on his—pouty and full. I'd never quench my want for them. The kiss was exquisite, then Rory wrapped his hand around my waist and pulled me to him, igniting an entirely new fire in us both. We stayed there, our desires vibrating between us—my hands in safe positions. But like before, Rory retracted and jumped back from me.

"I'm sorry," he whispered.

"I'm not." I smiled at him. "That kiss was amazing."

"But what if that's all I can ever give you?"

"Then I will be a very lucky bear because I could live on kisses like that."

Rory's cheek lifted in a half-smile. "You'll get bored with me."

I held out my hands for him, and Rory took them. I wish I were brave enough to tell him I was in love with him. But I wasn't sure if he was there yet. I didn't want to push him.

"You're more likely to get bored with me. Are you sure you want to get involved with a mature bear like me? I might drag your youth down to my level."

Now, I got a full smile from Rory.

"Never."

"Then we'll leave it at that."

Rory sighed. "Goodnight, Denver."

I took a chance and kissed his forehead. "We'll make more plans." I reluctantly released his hands as I walked backward and then turned to jog down the steps.

Rory was leaning against the railing, watching me as I headed off for my truck. Before I reached it, I took off Jesse's sweatpants and wrapped them around a thorny bush.

I hoped they stank of me.

My torn clothes retrieved from beside my truck, I pictured Rory's crimson lips and soulful eyes as I drove off. I wanted to stare at them forever.

No matter what he'd done or had done *to* him—I wanted forever with him.

If he'd have me.

CHAPTER 13

RORY

The night shift was truly work today. And I didn't want to be here. I'd had three days off in a row, and Denver and I spent much of it together. Those days and the last two weeks had been magical.

We'd taken to shifting near his home so we could cuddle, uninterrupted by my overly protective roommates. We usually ended up on Denver's sofa, but we'd also used his bed.

Being on Denver's bed with him had made me feel a little uncomfortable at first, but I soon grew to love it. We always kept our pants on, but I was getting used to being upper body skin on skin with him, my back pressed against his hairy chest, his lips kissing the back of my head.

Sometimes when we woke after a nap, Denver's cock would be hard and prodding against my ass. The first time it happened, I panicked and leapt off the bed, memories flooding my mind.

The next time, I took a string of long, even breaths and remembered that *Denver* was behind me, and he would never hurt me or make me do something I didn't want to do.

It was his body's natural waking response and nothing more.

"Can you run the food to table five?" Jonas asked as he sped past me. We were getting slammed. I liked it when it was busy. But I'd like it better if I were with Denver.

I went into the kitchen and grabbed two plates of roast dinner for table five. I was halfway across the restaurant when a familiar, putrid scent wafted over me, invading my nostrils.

The dishes I was carrying crashed onto the floor at my feet, and I froze in place—shattered ceramic and hot food all over the tiles, my senses becoming acute, but I couldn't move.

How the hell had they found me?

The threat of danger made my adrenaline kick up.

Come on, Rory ... think.

A shiver ran up my spine, and I catapulted into survival mode. Once regaining my ability to think and reason, I whipped around. Standing inside the front door were my dad and uncle.

Looming large and ugly. And they were staring straight at me.

Jonas rushed to my side. "Are you all right?"

I shook my head, unable to speak; I was so petrified. When they started walking toward me, I grabbed Jonas and practically climbed in behind him.

"Can I help you, gentlemen?" Jonas asked them, quickly catching on that they were the problem—that the floor was covered in broken plates, roast beef, gravy, and veg because of them.

"No," my dad answered. "We're here for Rory."

Jonas crossed his arms. "Why?"

My uncle stepped forward. "We're his family ... and we miss him."

The rumble started low in Jonas' chest. He knew something was up, but he was half their size. He couldn't possibly protect me from them. "He's busy. You can see him after his shift."

My dad tsked and shook his head. "No ... see, that wouldn't be good enough."

"He needs to come with us now," my uncle added.

Jonas splayed his arms back like a swan to keep me contained behind him. I was going to owe him my life if we managed to get me out of what I knew might be coming.

My uncle lunged first and put a stranglehold on my arm. To his credit, Jonas growled and snapped at him. But it was of no use. My uncle had a firm grip on me. He pulled me from my hiding spot and yanked me away from Jonas' reach. My dad grabbed my other arm.

"Denver!"

"You were difficult to track down," my dad said.

"If it weren't for a bike we wanted to sell for parts, we never would have found you."

My mind scurried through how that had led them to Creekside. Then I remembered the photo of my boss and me that he kept on the corkboard behind the desk. They must have seen it.

I hung my head down. My boss was unaware of my background. He would have unwittingly told my dad and uncle that I had moved to Creekside after they identified themselves as my family.

The sound of whining filled the room.

I hadn't expected Jonas to shift in the middle of his restaurant, but he did. After ripping his clothes away, his full wolf came out, and he charged at my dad, teeth gnashing the air.

One backhand from my uncle, and Jonas skidded across the floor on his back.

"Denver!"

That's when the terror really set in. My dad and uncle hauled me toward the door. My uncle took the opportunity to sniff the side of my neck. I convulsed as my skin crawled, ready to throw up. Then my legs gave out. They hauled me back up and dragged me forward.

My dad kicked open the door, and they pulled me outside.

I should be fighting against them to free myself. But they'd conditioned me well. Fighting them meant more pain later. My body and mind wanted to avoid that at all costs.

My uncle opened their car door, and they started shoving me toward the dark space beyond. Some part of me resisted. I locked my legs and leaned backward.

"Denver!"

"Don't give us any trouble." My dad clung to the back of my neck and bent me forward, throwing me off balance. I stumbled, almost landing face-first on the backseat. "We have so many plans for you when we get you back home, don't we, Tom?"

"We certainly do." My uncle bent my arm behind my back. "In!"

"Denver!"

There was a tremendous, ear-splitting roar, and then my uncle disappeared, yanked off my arm, and I felt fur shoving me aside. I would recognize that scent anywhere.

My Denver had come for me.

Within seconds, I could smell blood.

"Who the fuck?" My dad jerked me back from the car and sped toward the door of Growlers with me in tow. He was stronger than I was, but I made it difficult for him. I shuffled along behind him, the sound of snarling, roaring, and thudding blows being exchanged in the dark near to us.

We burst through the doors and into the central part of the restaurant. Jonas was standing naked behind the counter with his eyes closed. His canines were protruding.

His eyes snapped open when he sensed us.

"You'd better leave him alone and get out of here." Jonas rumbled as he spoke. "I've called for reinforcements and believe me ... you do *not* want to mess with my entire pack."

My dad produced a knife from a sheath on his hip and held it to my throat.

"Either he comes with us, or his life ends right here."

His stance and words caused panic in the restaurant. The already distressed patrons rushed for the doors, some screaming, as they all pushed and shoved to get away from what was unfolding.

Jonas held up his hands. "Let him go. Just let him live his life in peace."

My dad snarled. "But the men in the sex club all *miss* him."

To his credit, Jonas didn't even blink. He was on my side no matter what. So was Denver. And apparently, the entire East Creekside wolf pack. I straightened up and started a rumble in my throat.

Before I had a chance to wrench myself away, the front doors exploded into splinters, shattered glass flying everywhere, and Denver sped, roaring his way in to where I was being held.

Denver didn't stop to consider for a second; he reared up and charged, not allowing my dad time to shift. Blood sprayed me in the face as the claws on Denver's right paw opened my dad's stomach, spilling the entirety of his entrails at his feet. He looked shocked before he collapsed.

One blow. That's all it had taken to end my nightmare.

The scent of wolves wafted in through the broken front door. At least twenty of them jogged in to survey what was left to be done. And one male human, carrying a shotgun.

They'd all come to my rescue.

Jonas raced over to the human and leapt into his arms. They were obviously mates, judging by the way they clutched and kissed. My mind wandered away from them.

I clutched my head, reeling—dizzy, and the room disappeared near the corners of my eyes. Everything was fading to black. I felt myself crumple.

Then nothing.

I woke to Denver patting my face and calling my name.

"Rory ... oh, thank god." His brow was creased, and his mouth turned down as his face hovered above me. "You fainted. You're not hurt, I checked. Can you sit up?"

I touched his face. His jaw, chin, lips, and nose were covered in blood. Then I remembered how Denver had attacked my uncle outside near the car, and judging by the amount of blood, my uncle was as dead as Denver had left my dad. "Are they both gone?" I asked to be sure.

"They'll never bother you again," Jonas said off to my other side.

I took a few shuddering breaths, then broke down in tears. Jonas moved away, and Denver stroked the hair that was stuck to my forehead. "I'm here, Rory. Right here for you."

"Still not running?"

Denver smiled at me. "Not in a million years."

My chest expanded with a sliver of joy. It only blocked out what had transpired for a brief second. A rush of anxiety had me grasping Denver's outstretched hand and using his strength to sit myself up. The room swam for a few seconds, but Denver helped me keep my balance.

"I was so scared." I rested my forehead on his shoulder. "How did you know I needed you?"

He cupped the back of my neck. "You were screaming for me."

"I don't remember that." I didn't remember much of what had happened.

"Luckily, I was in town buying something."

He heard me calling him.

The connection between Denver and me, even after almost two months, sometimes felt surreal. "And you came for me." I still had trouble believing it. My dad and uncle were dead. The source of my nightmares had been reached by karma at last—in the form of my Denver.

I pulled back and cradled his jaw. I didn't care that he was nude and covered in blood. I kissed him like no one was watching. Deep and appreciative—and loving.

He loved me. I knew he did.

And I loved him right back.

"Take me home," I whispered against his lips.

"Should we call Carter and Jesse first, so we don't just show up like this?"

I shook my head. "No. Your home. I need to be *there* with you."

"Wherever you need to be, we'll go."

I nodded and clutched Denver's bare arm. Once outside, we walked to the far end of Main Street where his truck was parked. On the pavement beside it, Denver's shredded clothes.

There'd be no point in trying to put them back on. I fixed my attention on Denver's muscular back, down to his ass, and his powerful thighs until he rounded the back of the truck.

I didn't mind him being naked. I loved my Alpha's body.

My Alpha.

The corner of my mouth lifted in an almost smile.

The ride to Denver's was quiet. He was giving me time to think about everything that had happened. To process the death of my dad and uncle. I appreciated him giving me a moment.

It would be a huge adjustment, not having to worry about them coming for me and hauling me back into that life with them. Me locking myself in my room every night to stay safe from them. I tipped my head against the cool glass of the window and let my tears flow.

Denver reached for my hand, and I welcomed the embrace of it.

He was showing me what I already knew. We were in this together.

Inside his home, we went into the downstairs bathroom, and Denver retrieved a first aid kit from under the sink. I motioned for him to sit on the toilet and went to work dressing his wounds. My fingers focused on new places. I was used to seeing him naked but not touching him. I had only caressed his face, furry chest, arms, and strong hands. I concentrated on my efforts.

My uncle had only landed a few strikes on Denver, and they were shallow enough that they didn't need stitches. The bite near his shoulder might require a course of antibiotics, though.

When I finished, I turned to the sink to wash my hands. In the mirror, I saw Denver step up behind me. He looked at me with so much love, I reached back for him to come closer.

I hummed as his hips pressed against me, and I clung to his hands when he wrapped his arms around my waist. I looked at us in the mirror. Despite the height difference, we fit.

"Can I kiss your neck?" he asked.

I held my breath for a second, then nodded my head.

I closed my eyes as his lips caressed the base of my neck. A single lingering kiss that ended far too soon. I wanted more of his touch. He would never hurt me. I needed to remember that.

"Make me feel good," I whispered, hoping he caught on to what I meant.

Denver stared at my eyes in the mirror. "Are you sure?"

"Never surer." I turned in his arms and cupped his face. "You complete me in ways I never thought imaginable. I need us to take this step in our relationship."

Denver bent forward and kissed me. Soft and languishing until he dragged himself away from my lips. "You're precious to me, Rory. I'll go at your speed. If you want me to stop, I'll stop."

I moved my hands from his face, down and around to his back, then traced his spine and ended on his ass. And hung on to ground myself. He shifted his hips and bare semi-hard cock forward.

I could feel it, but I didn't fear it.

I moaned and grasped his face again, pulling him down onto my lips. He tipped me backward in a desperate bid to get closer to me. I placed my hand on his chest. "Let's go upstairs."

He gripped my shoulders gently. "Are you sure this is the right time?"

I moved him a step back. "You've chased off my nightmares, asleep and awake. Those bears you killed tonight weren't my family. Not really. I was an object to them."

"I get that, but shouldn't you spend some time processing what happened today?"

I ran my fingers along his jawline. "I will ... but right now, I need you. You are the best thing that has ever happened to me." I rose and gave him a quick kiss. "Please, Denver."

The details of my dad and uncle's deaths would slowly come back online. I would make space for those memories when they did appear. Deal with them and then file them away.

Right now, though, I only wanted thoughts of Denver.

Others had come to my rescue because Jonas called them. Jonas had stood his ground because he cared for me like an Omega mama bear.

But Denver ... I could see it in his eyes.

He'd come because he *loved* me.

My wounded spirit wanted a deeper connection with him. My body ached for him. I'd never longed for someone's loving touch before. Not lewd touch—but all encompassing intimate love.

Denver closed his bedroom door behind us and locked it—for my peace, not for any need of his. Even though I knew my dad and uncle weren't out there anymore, it would take me a while.

"Do you want me to undress you?" Denver asked.

I stared at the floor. "I'd rather do it myself."

"You don't need to be embarrassed by that." Denver appeared in front of me, placed his finger under my chin, and lifted my head. I met his gaze. Warmth radiated from his eyes to mine.

"I'm not embarrassed. I'm just not used to it being my choice."

Denver dragged his knuckles softly along my cheek. "*Everything* is your choice, Rory."

My choice.

I kept my attention on his eyes as I removed my hoodie. It was my barrier against the world. I didn't need it here. Denver took it from me and laid it on the end of the bed. My threadbare shirt was next. Even more than my hoodie, I didn't need it to protect me.

I turned toward the bed and set my shirt on my hoodie. I kept my back to Denver as I unbuttoned and unzipped my pants. I could hear my heartbeat thudding between my ears as I fumbled with them. The enormity of what I was doing hit me as I let them drop to the floor and kicked them aside with my feet. I hesitated, made a choice, and kept my underwear in place.

My breathing lightened as I turned back, and Denver held me in his gentle gaze. I searched my heart to be sure of my choice. I *wasn't* ready to remove any more of my clothing.

And Denver seemed all right with that.

"So beautiful ...." Denver stepped into my space and held my face in both hands. Slowly and deliberately, he took his time as he brought his lips onto mine.

I pushed my fingers through the hair on his pecs and pressed into his flesh. Each kiss dove deeper, growing hungrier and more passionate. I needed to taste him. For the first time in my life, I slipped my tongue into someone's mouth. Denver allowed me to explore without reciprocating.

I moved my hands onto Denver's hips and tugged on him as I walked backward until the back of my thighs were against the mattress. I sat and put my hands behind me to support myself.

I reluctantly pulled away from Denver's mouth.

His gorgeous lashes hid and revealed his eyes as he watched me.

My Alpha was waiting for me to make another choice.

I relinquished my support and lay flat on the bed. "I need your lips on my body."

Denver growled softly, then turned my head to one side. He started by laying a line of kisses down my jawline, ending at my ear, his stubble roughing up my skin. He kissed my earlobe, then turned to my neck. One kiss after another until he reached my shoulder, and I was trembling.

"Other side?" he asked.

I licked my lips, nearly vibrating out of my skin. "Please."

This time, I was ready and allowed my body to immerse itself fully in the experience. I hummed and closed my eyes, soaking in every moment. A vacuum appeared as he finished his last kiss and withdrew from my shoulder. I opened my eyes.

"Where would you like me to go next?" Denver asked as he stroked my face.

I swallowed. "My chest. Maybe my abs."

"If I get to your abs and it's too much, don't hesitate to stop me."

The most I could manage was a nod.

Denver started with my collarbones, then trailed down the center of my chest, one kiss after another. I pushed my hand into his hair and directed him to my left nipple.

He looked up at me. "Are you sure?"

A flash of memory of all the males who had sucked on my nipples made a brief appearance in my mind. I dismissed every single one of them. I dragged a breath in and out. "Yes."

The attention he gave me immediately felt different. Denver gently suckled on it, reverent, whereas those other males had sucked and bit my nipples to hurt me.

I gripped his hair and pressed him to me to let him know I was enjoying it. With each suck and lash of his tongue, a tingle went from my nipple straight down to my dick.

I rolled my hips up and moved my hands to his back.

He switched nipples, then kissed the crest of my abs. My hands slipped to his shoulders as he dropped to his knees at the foot of the bed. I held my breath as he kissed his way to my soft belly, his chin pressing against my pubic bone. He caressed my thighs as he looked into my eyes.

"Hip bones," I said.

He smiled at me. "With pleasure."

Denver didn't just kiss them—he sucked on them. The sensation was beyond exquisite. I moaned, and my body instinctively thrust my hips up. He hummed in appreciation, but then stood, his stunning cock erect. I drew my attention away from it. Denver had stopped because he knew I wouldn't want him to go lower. He was handling me with such care and respect.

"Shimmy up the bed?" he asked.

I smiled at him. "With pleasure." Copying him.

I scooted up the bed until my head was on a pillow. Denver kneeled on the bed to either side of my legs, then crawled toward me. He reached my mouth, and our lips reunited.

Such hunger.

The kisses were more desperate this time—our absolute desire surfacing.

"Can I put my weight on you?" he asked when we came up for air.

"We can try, but take it slow."

Slower than slow, Denver lowered his body onto mine. There was a moment of panic when I first felt compressed against the mattress. It passed when Denver whispered my name.

Surprising myself, I broke my legs free from under him and wrapped them around his waist. I placed my hands on his lower back, then his ass, jamming his hard cock against mine.

Denver groaned and pressed his eyes shut.

Even on the escalation of fulfillment, I knew Denver would stop here if I asked him to. I had no intention of doing that. I thrust my hips and ground against him while squeezing his ass. He got the message and started a slow undulation, rubbing our dicks together through my underwear.

His cock would be weeping; he was so turned on. I was right there with him, my shaft hardening with each pass. I clung tighter to him and encouraged him to speed up.

I closed my eyes and tipped my head back, nearly driving my chest off the mattress. Denver's breath was hot on my cheek. He grew increasingly louder. His grunting almost threw me off.

A brief flash of my dad and uncle being noisy behind me burst in.

"Shh ...," I whispered in his ear.

He was immediately quiet.

My undulations became frantic, matching every one of Denver's thrusts. My gut tightened, and I felt my balls lift. I brought Denver's face back to kiss me.

So close.

There ... right there.

We both groaned, lips sealed, as we released the sexual tension between us as one. I was floating high, euphoric, until I imagined Denver's cum on my skin.

I clenched my eyes closed, trying to erase the invasive memory of lying on the floor with a ring of men standing around me, cumming all over me.

I grabbed Denver's shoulders and pressed on them.

"You want me off?" he asked.

Tears pooled in my eyes. My past had destroyed a beautiful moment with Denver. I wasn't sure I'd ever be able to banish the unwelcome thoughts. "I just need a minute."

Denver rolled off me and lay beside me, staying on his side, watching me. I didn't want him to see me crying, but I knew he needed to witness my anguish. It was part of sharing with him.

"What happened?" he asked.

"Bukkake scene." I decided to be honest with him.

"You at the center of it?"

"I can taste it and feel it stinging my eyes. Wearing it on my face, in my hair, and covering my junk while they fucked me. The messier I was, the more they liked it."

Denver touched my face and turned it to him. "Never again, Rory. I promise you that." Then he pushed himself up. "Let me get a hot cloth so you can clean yourself." He left the bed and disappeared into the ensuite bathroom. He emerged a few seconds later with a wet washcloth.

I put my hands on my chest, indicating I wanted him to wash his cum off my skin. He wiped and refolded the cloth a few times until he was satisfied that my belly was clean.

I wasn't sure what to do about the mess I'd made in my underwear.

Trust him.

"You can pull off my underwear."

Denver's eyebrows rose as he stared at me. "Are you absolutely sure?"

"I trust you."

Delicately, my Alpha stripped my underwear off my hips, then drew them down my legs, and dispensed with them onto the floor at the foot of the bed.

It's not like he'd never seen my dick before. Every time we shifted, it was on display. Never like this, though. On his bed, covered in my fresh cum.

Denver cleared his throat. "Let me rinse this out and get it hot again." Then he went back into the bathroom. When he returned, he held out the cloth for me to take.

I had a choice to make.

It was a surprisingly easy one.

I shook my head. "No, you can do it."

I could tell Denver was struggling with his breathing as he ran the cloth along the top of my dick and balls. He would need to get more hands-on to clean them properly.

Gingerly, my Alpha lifted my soft cock away from my balls and wiped it, then moved it aside and did a better job of cleaning my sacs, cradling them gently in his palm.

I'd never felt so cared for.

Denver finished, put the washcloth aside, and joined me at the head of the bed. He arranged his arms for me, and I found my place. The place I felt most safe.

The thick hair on his chest was like a soft pillow for my cheek. My face and hand rode every breath he took. I wrapped my leg over his, not pulling back when my cock touched his hip.

Denver stroked my head until my breathing descended into being shallow.

"I loved what we did," Denver said.

I kissed his pec. "Me too."

He buried his face into my hair, then his breath slowed. When he started snoring softly, I felt at peace. This was where I belonged. Here in his home—in his bed—in his arms.

I slept peacefully. Denver and I were running through the trees. Sometimes as bears. Sometimes in our human form. Running and free. Falling into the grass and holding one another.

Deeply in love.

CHAPTER 14

DENVER

R ory, stirring beside me, woke me. He moved jerkily, then repositioned himself, tucked tightly against my side. He kissed my chest and started playing with my chest hair.

"I'm ready to share something," he said.

"I'm ready to listen."

His hand curled into a fist, and his body tensed. The morning sun shone through my window, giving me a clear view down his naked side. Even his leg tightened on mine.

"Only if you're sure you're ready," I said; his body was sending other signals.

Rory traced his fingers along my collarbone. "Just hear me out to the end."

I kissed his head.

"When I was about thirteen, things changed for me." His hand stopped moving. "My dick started getting hard when they played with me."

I felt a wave of sadness. I hoped Rory didn't hate himself for that.

"Even when they tied me up in the backyard and left me swinging in the cool night air, I couldn't stop my body ... and over time my mind from enjoying it."

I swallowed.

Rory.

"They used to flog and whip me out there until I couldn't stop the tears. The pain was so intense, I used to whimper. No one cared that the neighbors might hear us. It added to the whole dirtiness of the experience." Rory was practically wearing a hole in my skin with his fingernail.

"I ...." Rory sighed, then sucked in a breath. "I grew to like it ... to love it."

Oh, my sweet Rory.

I held his head and peppered kisses on his hair. The last thing I would ever do is judge him for what his mind and body had enjoyed, despite the source of that pleasure.

"And then they introduced me to sex clubs. Some of it, I hated, like being painted in cum. But the rest of it ...." He puffed a breath past my nipple. "I loved being fucked by multiple men."

And then he was quiet.

"Still not running," I said.

"*I* did."

"What do you mean?"

"One of the men said something that snapped me out of it. We were doing a humiliation scene. I was kneeling at his feet, and he was ...." Rory stopped and shook his head. "He called me a nasty little cunt boy. The impact of his words struck me. I knew I needed to escape that life.

"I ran away to the back alleys of Metro City. I was fifteen, and I was scared. I only knew how to do one thing to make money to buy food. Be on my knees ... and I was good at it."

Rory stopped for a moment. I knew he wasn't done yet.

"My boss found me behind a pub, servicing a desheveled old human male. He hauled me to my feet and told me he had a job for me. That's where I learned to work on bikes and skateboards."

I took in a long breath.

If I ever met that man, I would thank him profusely for rescuing my Rory.

"He let me sleep in the backroom of the shop until I had enough money to rent an apartment. When I did, it wasn't much, but it provided me with some semblance of safety and security."

"Is that when you met Carter and Jesse?"

"No, I met them when I was still sleeping in doorways. Finding other bears felt as if we were destined to be together. We used to huddle in the rain at night, a drop sheet over our heads."

I clutched my chest. It felt as though a spear had been plunged through my heart. Tears gathered in my eyes. Rory's increasingly matter-of-fact tone struck a deep chord within me.

"Jesse was in and out of prison, but during his first time inside, Carter had the idea that we needed to move to the forest. We worked hard to save money. Jesse made up his share when he was out, stealing more stuff and having sex with as many males as he could manage.

"Carter *dated*, too. I would have, but after being away from that life, I developed a fear of people touching me. After about a year, the slightest touch from anyone brought me right back to when I was still a young child, when my dad and uncle used to handle and invade my body."

Rory shivered and started trembling. His brave tone had collapsed. He clung tighter to me and buried his face against my shoulder. The memories were breaking past his restraints.

"I'm here for you." What else could I say? He'd shared so much. He hadn't done it so I could ask lots of questions about his life. He simply wanted me to know.

His hot breath came in gusts against my skin as he began to weep. I couldn't hold back. I tugged him to me and let my tears flow with his. We became a whimpering, sobbing mass.

Rory for recent events, the suffering he'd endured, and the guilt he felt.

Me, because the bear I loved had been robbed of his innocence.

The weeping turned to Rory grasping my face and kissing me—hard and fast, like he hoped to forget by fervently attacking me. It wasn't the way for either of us to wipe our minds.

I held Rory's face and pulled away from his lips. "Rory, stop."

Rory's expression turned pained, and he struggled out of my arms.

"You don't want me anymore."

"God, Rory ...." I reached for his hand, and thank god, he didn't recoil. He let me hold his in mine. "Of course, I want you. Your past doesn't change that."

"What if I'm a sexual deviant?"

"Do you honestly believe that? I know plenty of folks who enjoy those things."

"It doesn't put you off that I liked being filled with load after load of cum?"

I grunted. Rory was trying to scare me off again. "It doesn't change how I feel about you." I brought his hand to my lips and kissed his fingers. Rory studied my face like he didn't believe me.

I blinked when his voice appeared in my mind.

"You're sure."

"More than everything else in my life."

His brow dipped. *"Do you think we're fated?"*

"I do. We're able to communicate without a word being spoken. We spend time together in each other's dreams. I don't know what else to call it, but that's more than wolves can do."

Rory came back to me and snuggled against me. *"You're my Alpha."*

"My beautiful Omega." I snuffled my nose against his head, inhaling his intoxicating scent. *"Promise me, you'll stop trying to push me away, because it isn't going to work."*

"I'll stop." Rory kissed my cheek. "But only if you feed me. I'm starving."

"Mm ... I have a load of bacon with both our names on it."

Rory sat up. "Perfect." Then he slipped off the bed. "No offense to your cleaning capabilities, but I'm going to have a shower while you get breakfast going."

I must have frowned.

"You could join me in the shower first," he said.

I clambered off the bed with such haste that it made Rory smile. He led the way into the bathroom and poked through my abundance of shampoos as I started and adjusted the water.

"Why so many?" Rory asked as he twisted open and sniffed one of them.

"My hair is complex."

He smiled at me. "*You're* complex. One of the things I love about you." Then he looked at the floor. Had he meant to use that word? Love. Did he love me? Before I could broach what he'd potentially revealed, Rory hurried under the water and started rumbling with pleasure.

He was right. Now wasn't the time.

I picked a shampoo and poured some into my hand. Rory was well under the flow of water, soaking wet, so I guided him back and started washing his hair.

He moaned and reached for the wall to steady himself. I gave him what I considered to be an epic scalp massage. He agreed because he turned around, pushed me up against the tiles on the far side of the shower, and attacked my mouth, kissing me until rivulets of shampoo and water from his hair ran into his eyes. It must have burned. I'm not sure why it was funny, but he pulled back laughing, and tears welled up in my eyes. I'd never seen him laugh outside of our dreams before.

My heart felt lighter after everything he had told me.

As he rinsed the shampoo from his hair and off his face, oblivious to my emotional reaction, I placed my hands on his hips. His skin was slick and soft. I used my thumbs to caress his spine, then my fingertips to explore the difference in texture of his many circular scars.

I suddenly realized he'd stopped moving.

He turned to face me.

"I'm ready," he whispered. "I want to feel you in me."

My brain shorted out, then I reconnected the circuit. "Not here ... not like this." Rory deserved more than to be taken from behind against a wall. He'd likely had enough of that in his life.

Rory changed gears.

"Let's finish our shower and get something to eat." He reached for the soap and lathered up his body, then handed it back to me. I took the soap and spent a second adjusting my expectation of events while I cleaned myself. We alternated under the spray until we were done.

I couldn't look away as he dried himself. First, his arms, chest, and back. Then around his hips and ass. All his private bits. Every so gently. Then he bent forward to do his legs and feet.

He'd caught me staring early on and given me a shy, one-sided smile. For the briefest of moments, I imagined all the men who had gazed upon his nudity. What had been going through their perverted minds as they leered at someone far too young for their sexual gratification?

I took my towel and roughed up my skin, I went so hard on it as I attempted to catch up to Rory. He left the bathroom ahead of me. When I emerged, he was dressed.

"I'll meet you downstairs," he said, then unlocked the door. He looked over his shoulder at me. "Thanks for locking it. I can't sleep unless I know my room is secure."

Then he was gone.

I remembered the lock on his bedroom door. As a child, he'd probably wished for a locking door to keep his dad and uncle out. Now, as an adult, he was able to provide that for himself.

I took my time getting dressed. I needed to think. Rory wanted to have sex with me. Not simply rubbing off on one another. He wanted me inside him. What should I expect?

Was he going to panic? Was he going to zone out?

Was my love for him going to be evident?

I looked at his underwear, discarded on the floor. He'd allowed me to clean off his skin. That had required a level of trust I hadn't expected him to be capable of achieving—maybe ever.

The smell of bacon cooking reached my nose. He'd started making breakfast without me. I jogged down the stairs and into the kitchen. He was wearing one of my barbecue aprons.

He looked adorable.

Freshly scrubbed, and his hair, untamed, standing over my stove, pushing bacon around in the grease it was creating. He had a carton of eggs on the counter that he kept touching, then retreating from. I suspected he might need some help coordinating the timing of cooking them.

And he'd started cooking without going out for a cigarette first. I wondered if he'd quit. He hadn't tasted like cigarettes when I kissed him last night. I wondered what had prompted that.

"I'll start some toast," I said. "Lift the bacon out when it's done onto a plate."

"And the eggs?"

"They only take a couple of minutes. I'll do them once the toast is ready."

Rory looked over his shoulder at me. "I grew up on cereal when we had it. We didn't always have milk. Then my dad went on a kick of buying raw oats for a while. Didn't cook them, though."

"So, you ate uncooked oats?"

Rory returned his attention to the bacon. "They're not bad, actually. Kinda chewy."

I put four slices of bread in the toaster. Rory's days of hunger were over.

"My dad would put my dish on the floor near his feet."

The butter knife in my hand clattered to the floor. Rory turned around. There was resolve in his gaze. He wanted to tell me everything. I needed to be strong for him.

He returned to the stove and flipped the bacon over. "After my tenth birthday, I wasn't allowed to eat with my hands. And I had to be naked at his feet, or I wouldn't eat at all."

Bile rose in my throat.

Sick fucking bastard.

I had to steady myself on the counter by placing one hand on it. Rory left the bacon and went in search of a plate. I couldn't speak to tell him which cupboard. He didn't look to me for help. He knew what he was telling me would be incapacitating me. Surely, he had to know.

The toast popped, and when I didn't go over to it, Rory set the plate he'd located beside the stove and went in search of the butter, another knife, and a cutting board, and found them quickly.

I felt as if I were looking through a haze as he finished making the bacon and toast.

How had he endured so much and not been completely broken?

How could he be speaking as if these things happened to someone else?

I needed to move.

On autopilot, I cooked the fried eggs. I didn't ask if Rory liked them sunny side up. My voice was still caught in my throat, and I assumed he wouldn't care how his eggs were cooked.

Dished up, I carried our plates to the kitchen dining table. Rory removed my apron and slid into a seat, his eyes wide, his fingers flexing to get started.

I brought some cutlery over, and that was it. Rory dug in, piling the food into his mouth as fast as he could. I slipped a piece of my toast and a strip of bacon onto his empty plate once he was finished. He peered up at me, then devoured what I had given him.

While I ate, Rory took his dishes to the sink and started washing them. I almost told him I had a dishwasher for that, but I didn't want to embarrass him and discount his efforts. He seemed particularly focused on doing a good job, scrubbing the plate to within an inch of its life.

He would've been punished if he'd failed in the task.

Probably even if he didn't fail.

"Is there anything you want to ask me?" Rory rinsed the plate and set it in the drying rack.

I had one question.

"How did you manage to survive it?"

Rory shrugged as he cleaned his fork. "Stubborn, I guess."

Stubborn, courageous, and strong. The bear I loved was a gladiator.

His fork and knife spotless and in the holder on the drying rack, Rory folded the dishcloth and set it on the back corner of the sink. He patted it as if to make sure it wouldn't move.

"I saw a puzzle in the living room."

We were changing subjects. I struggled to catch up. The image of Rory eating off a plate on the floor kept battering its way into my mind. Nude with his face covered in food.

Fuck.

"Yeah, I started it yesterday."

"Can I give it a try? I haven't done a puzzle in a long time."

"You're welcome to it."

Rory turned and smiled at me. Not one of his shy smiles. It was the kind of smile that reached his eyes. He was happy. He'd shared those stories and come away delighted about a puzzle.

"I'll meet you out there," I said and took my plate to the sink. When I was sure he was in the living room, I opened the dishwasher, then thought better of it and washed my dishes by hand.

I found him kneeling on the floor by the coffee table, scanning through the pieces I'd only managed to sort and turn face up. I had been one piece short of completing the border.

Rory had already found it and slotted it into place. I sat on the sofa behind him and enjoyed the sight of his mind working in what amounted to play. It sounded as though he'd had very little of that in his young life. I wanted to know how I could support him—to help him thrive.

"Rory ...."

"Mm-hm." He didn't look away from the puzzle.

"What do you need from me?"

He looked over his shoulder at me. "What do you mean?"

I hoped to avoid struggling with my words. "If you'll have me, I want to be your shelter ... the person you can turn to ... I need to know how best to do that for you."

Rory swivelled completely and sat on the carpet. "You represent safety and security for me already. You have since the first day I met you, and you called to me to come back to you after my dumpster diving introduction. After just one meeting, you showed genuine care for me. I knew right then that you were someone I might trust someday." He bit his bottom lip, deep in thought, then placed his hands on my knees. "What I *do* need from you *now* is patience."

My heart skittered.

"Have I not been giving that to you?"

"Denver, yes." Rory rose to his feet, climbed onto the sofa, and straddled my legs. He ran his hands through my hair above my ears. "Yes, you have. You've been perfect."

I released a long sigh, emptying my lungs, and inhaled slowly through my nose as Rory caressed my mouth with his lips, and I chased everything he was offering.

I would never grow tired of kissing Rory.

He felt like the home I'd never thought to build for myself. The home that was perfect for me and Rory. A home we could both live in. I pulled away and held his face.

He was so breathtakingly beautiful—inside and out.

I was deeply in love with him.

Rory saw it in my eyes.

He placed his forehead on mine and whispered *I love you, too* on my lips.

Chapter 15

RORY

The words were out. Words I never thought I would whisper to anyone. Denver and I were in love. He was my Alpha, and I was his Omega. Whether we were fated mates or not, we had cultivated our love over time, despite my history of sexual abuse, sex work, and guilty desire.

Denver didn't judge me for any of it. He loved me, and I trusted him.

I trusted him with my life.

Because he had saved mine.

I groaned as Denver's hands moved from my back onto my ass, encouraging me to grind my cock against him. Up and back, my hands in his hair, devouring his mouth.

I tangled my tongue with his, skimming past his teeth, then retreated. I gripped his hair tighter and straightened up, thrusting my stiffened shaft against his chest.

Then I opened my mouth and whimpered.

Denver got the message.

He was careful and gentle as he slipped his tongue into my mouth. I welcomed him, my tongue lazy as I played with his. It wasn't an invasion. I'd extended an invitation.

The memory of my dad nearly choking me with his tongue flitted into my mind, not as a waking nightmare but a mere observation. Now that he and my uncle were dead, my mind had shifted. I wasn't afraid of it happening again anymore. I was working toward being free of them.

I hoped one day I would feel liberated. Telling Denver about my dad's method of feeding me had come out of my mouth like a simple conversation might. No emotion. No reliving it.

They were dead, and I was coming to terms with that.

Denver gripped my ass and massaged it, his fingers splayed, moving with each thrust of my hips until one of his fingertips grazed the seam of my pants above my hole.

I felt myself go feral.

I panted against his lips as I pushed my ass toward his touch. He stroked the seam until stars appeared in front of my eyes. My cock was beyond aching.

I climbed off him. "Let's go upstairs."

He remained seated. "Slow down a second, Rory."

"Why?" I was so ready. My body was on fire.

"I need you to take a moment to consider where this is leading."

I furrowed my brow. "I already told you I'm ready."

"I know, but I wanted to check in."

My sweet, sweet Alpha.

I reached for his hands and encouraged him to his feet. "I need you to show me your love."

Denver grasped my head and kissed my forehead. "I *do* love you."

"Then I trust you."

Denver was a brute, which I loved, and scooped me up in his arms and carried me upstairs. Then he was a gentleman as he set me on my feet at the foot of the bed.

His constant rumbling growl of arousal filled the room.

He turned and locked the door, then took his time coming to me, his gaze running up and down my body. He cupped my jaw with his hand and brushed my cheek with his thumb.

He grew silent, taking me in.

"You are so beautiful."

I shifted on my feet. I wasn't good at accepting compliments. My young life had been full of them. Insincere words of praise. Words that were used to get me to do what they wanted.

Call me a good and pretty boy, and then fuck me.

Breathe.

Denver's palm was warm on my face as I burrowed into it.

My Alpha would only speak the truth to me.

I brushed my hands up his pecs to his shoulders, then around his neck. I sighed and felt myself relax as Denver wrapped his arms around me in a hug, which I hadn't realized I needed.

Moving apart, he descended onto my mouth, kiss after passionate kiss, nearly undoing me as I fought to give him more. I wanted to give him everything.

Every breath—every pulse in my veins.

I struggled to secure a grip on him that would bring him close enough, but failed time and again. He would need to crawl inside me for me to be satisfied. I tugged on his hips and closed my eyes, floating on the verge of losing all sense of reason as his hard dick rubbed against mine.

My hole clenched, wanting to be filled.

"Undress me," I murmured, barely able to speak.

Denver's fingers found the zipper on my hoodie and dragged it down. Once he had it undone, he lifted the material off my shoulders and then off my arms. I pulled my hands free.

The hoodie landed on a chair in the corner.

He touched my chin, angled my face up, and kissed me ever so softly, then grabbed the material at the bottom of my shirt and stripped it off over my head.

Onto the chair it went.

I could tell he was nervous when he started undoing my pants. His hands were trembling. I gave him a reprieve by tugging off his tight, grey shirt. Released from it, his hands went back to work, and before long, he was crouching in front of me, lifting my feet out of my pants.

He looked up at me, his eyes pleading with me like a bear cub looking for a treat.

Trust.

I ran my fingers through his hair and nodded.

Denver sank onto his knees and slipped his fingers into the band of my underwear. He drew them down to my ankles, and I stepped out of them.

He looked up at me again.

"Yes," I whispered, making my choice.

Denver cradled my balls in his hand, then nuzzled his nose in the crease of my groin and inhaled, then licked me there. It tickled, but I managed to stay still.

I grasped a handful of Denver's hair as he slathered my balls in saliva with his wet tongue, and sucked one into his mouth, savoring it, and humming, sending vibrations up my cock.

He made an appreciative sound before moving to my other sac. I adjusted my stance and placed my hands on his shoulders to steady myself. The sensation of being encased by Denver's mouth was glorious and all ours. I wallowed in it until he slurped and released my ball.

My dad appeared as Denver held my stiff cock and licked the pre-cum from my slit. I banished him, but not before I heard him tell me how good I tasted.

Stop it.

I closed my eyes and sank into the experience of Denver drawing my dick into his mouth and fondling it with his tongue. I grunted when he started to alternate pumping it within his fist and sucking and bobbing on my rock-hard length. Any longer and I would cum.

I touched his face. "Enough for now."

Denver huffed after he released me as if I had taken away his favorite toy. When he rose to his feet, I brought his lips down to mine to experience any remnants of what I tasted like.

Dirty, dirty boy.

Shut up.

I led Denver backward until my thighs were against his bed. I left his lips behind as I shuffled up the bed and watched Denver strip out of his jeans and boxers.

He was beyond gorgeous.

Denver crawled toward me and stopped for a second to check in with me before he layered his weight on me and used his mouth to draw out every desire I'd ever had. Tangled together, we squirmed and thrusted and panted each other's names, driving ourselves into a frenzy.

"Now, Denver ... I need you now." To emphasize my desperate need for him, I freed my legs from beneath him. "Let me roll over. Get my ass nice and high for you."

He frowned.

What did I do wrong?

My heart thundered, and a tinny sound reverberated in my ears.

What had I done to upset him?

"I'm not one of the males who would fuck you from behind." Denver stroked his fingers through the hair at my temple. "I love you, Rory. I want to see your face. To stare into your eyes. To see your shifting emotions as you become dismantled. To witness your love radiating up at me. I want to make love to you with every last measure of my deepest desire and devotion to you."

I swallowed, and tears gathered in the corners of my eyes.

I'd never been made love to before. My heart yearned for it. I wrapped my legs around his waist and gripped the back of his neck. I did my best to blink away the gathering tears.

Only one escaped.

Denver wiped it from my skin with his thumb as he cupped my face. "Only as far as you want to go. I have no expectations. We go at your speed and your speed only."

Then he gave me the sweetest, most sincere kiss.

It was pure love.

When I whispered *okay* against his lips, Denver stayed close but slid his finger into the slickness my channel was creating, in and out of my hole, sending shivers of pleasure up my spine.

He took his time, introducing more fingers at a pace that didn't hurt me.

Never hurt me. This was Denver, the bear I loved, treating me with such reverence, not rushing. Each thrust of his fingers felt nothing but pure and good—and destined.

He finished fingering me open and came in for another kiss, grounding us both before we embarked on something monumental. What was happening was more than touch.

Denver was about to be inside me.

The kiss ended, but Denver kept his lips hovering above mine, his eyes fixed on me as he fumbled between us. I gripped his back, sighing softly when I felt his cockhead at my hole.

He stopped. "Okay?"

"Yes," I murmured.

Denver pushed gently—slowly until my body accepted him, then drew him in.

He rested his forehead on mine. "Is this good ... are you all right?"

I bit my bottom lip and nodded.

Denver kissed me and angled his hips, gliding in further. I growled as he seated himself all the way inside me. I loved this feeling of fullness. But with Denver, my enjoyment took on meaning I'd never experienced in my life. I wanted him here because I loved him.

I'd never had that before.

Our intimacy wasn't purely sexual. We were in love.

"Still good?" he asked, because he was the sweetest, kindest, most caring bear I could have ever imagined would come into my life. I'd left Metro City and found my eternity Alpha.

"Yes." I kissed him, teasing and hungry, to let him know I meant it.

Denver shifted his hips back, withdrawing, breaking contact with my lips, then he caressed his cock into me. Sparks. Absolutely electrifying, colorful, energizing sparks lit up my body.

"Again." I shifted my ass.

His attention on my eyes, he did as I asked, retreating, then gliding up into me high but slow as if he wanted to stay inside me forever. Again and again, gently and sweetly.

"My Denver," I whispered, as I hugged him to me with my legs, then swam in the depths of euphoria as sensual pools of dark, chocolatey brown stared down at me.

It might have been the softness around the edges of his eyes, the way he blinked at me with his stunning lashes, the way his tongue darted out onto his lips, or some glint my subconscious was picking up, but I knew no one would ever love me as much as my Denver did.

I was his everything.

Maybe we *could* stay like this forever.

"Rory ...." Tears rimmed Denver's lower lids, and when he shuttered his eyes for a moment, fat droplets hit my cheeks. His breathing quickened, as if he was holding onto something.

I used my thumbs to clear the tears from under his eyes. "I feel it, too."

The earth had shifted. Time no longer made sense. The world was only right when we were together. More. The world had been at odds for all eternity until we found one another.

I cupped his face. "Love me, Denver ... please."

He started slowly, but then he grunted, and his rhythm changed, coming at me harder and quicker. He avoided going so far as to pummel me, but he was giving me what I needed.

Denver slipped his hand around my dick and pumped it. Every time he caressed my cockhead, his thumb slipped through the continuous flow of slick precum there.

Yes.

I groaned and undulated my hips up and back in time to his thrusts and the tightness of his grip on my dick. I didn't take my attention off his eyes. Each thrust, each jostle of the bed, we never looked away. It was the most intimate and sensual experience of my life.

The room melted away around us. It was only Denver and me—and him moving in me. Nothing had ever felt so real. I pressed my heels into his ass and guided him into our perfect pace.

There—right there.

Clinging to one another, Denver's cock throbbed and lifted inside me. One throaty roar, then he kissed me with an outpouring of fierce Alpha love as his body jerked.

I could feel each pulse as he filled me.

My balls and the base of my cock ached as I imagined Denver's cum inside of me. Coating my guts, ready to drip from my ass. I trembled and clutched Denver's shoulders.

I need to cum.

No.

I was suspended from a tree, my ass cheeks on fire, my cock being pumped.

Stop.

Fucking stop.

I dismissed it and returned to Denver.

He pulled away from my lips, and we regained our connection, watching the shifting expression in one another's eyes. Knowing what I needed, my Alpha stroked my dick until I arched my back, whimpering, and spilled onto my stomach while he guided me through it.

After my body calmed, Denver set a leisurely pace, gliding in and out of me until his cock softened and slipped free. I jammed my fingers in his hair, drawing him to my lips.

This is where I was now.

Everything happening was my reality, my life—my love.

Now, it was my turn to break down and cry. I never wanted to let Denver go. I wanted to stay in this snapshot of our lives forever. We were both reluctant when I released Denver from my leg's grasp, and he rolled off me. He landed heavily beside me, then opened his arms for me.

"Come to me, Omega."

I was quick to find my way into his embrace.

He kissed the top of my head. "I love you."

I smiled up at him. "I love you, too."

"You're all right?"

"I'm slightly overwhelmed, but I'm okay."

Denver brushed a few tears off my cheeks. "I'll cherish what we shared ... how you trusted me to make love to you. How you trusted me with your body and your mind."

I wasn't sure what to say. I stroked Denver's collarbone as I played with words in my mind. What we'd shared—I would carry the feel of his love with me forever. "I'll always trust you."

Denver snuggled me hard against him. "But you have to go, don't you?"

"Ugh." I had no idea what time it was, but knew it was fast approaching my shift at work. There was no way I would ever let Jonas down after what he'd done for me.

I wrinkled my nose.

"What do you think they did with the bodies? Are the police going to be involved?"

Denver laughed. I'm not sure why. "East Creekside wolf pack constitutes the police around here. Maddox will take one look at the circumstances and bury the bodies in the forest somewhere."

"The humans won't ask questions?"

"They know how things work here. The mayor is on the wolf pack's side." Denver chuckled. "Considering he's one of them." He patted my back. "I have nothing to worry about."

"I'd hate to have found my Alpha and then have him go down for a double murder."

"Not going to happen. We're bears handling our own business."

"Hm ... I'm going to trust you on that." I rolled away from him. "Here's me getting into the shower again." I stopped before I reached the door. "What time *is* it?"

Denver hoisted himself off the bed and retrieved his phone from his jeans.

"Ten past eleven."

"Shit. I work at one and I need to change my clothes."

"Let me crowd into that shower with you and then I'll drive you home."

"Solid plan if you behave."

I let Denver play with the water temperature, then stepped in ahead of him. I had more parts to clean than he did. On the trip to the bathroom, the inside of my thighs had become sticky with Denver's cum. He came like an Alpha—purpose-built for breeding and producing cubs.

Standing under the shower, I set my hand on my belly, wondering.

Now, at nineteen, I'd been through several heats; once every three months. Thinking of them always brought on feelings of anguish, and I was due for one soon.

I leaned back against Denver as he came up behind me and wrapped his arms around my waist. He kissed the curl of my ear. "What are you thinking about?"

"How I'm never going to get clean with you hovering all sexy behind me?"

Denver chuckled. "Give me the soap."

I lathered up my stomach and cock, then passed the bar back to him. I imagined where he was cleaning on his body. My hole clenched as I remembered his dick deep inside me.

He kissed my shoulder.

"Do you need help?" he whispered close to my ear.

I tipped my head back, resting it on his shoulder. "Please."

He traced a finger down my spine to my tailbone. "Here?"

"Lower."

I placed my hands on the tiles in front of me. Denver was gentle as he ran his soapy hand down my crack, washing it, then caressed my hole, his fingers lingering, then my balls, and between my thighs until they were clean. He stepped up close behind me. His cock on my skin was hard. He continued to touch me, massaging my ass cheeks, then moved one hand onto my hip.

Fuck.

My ass opened for him. I reached back and grabbed his hand, stopping him. "We're never going to get out of here if you keep that up."

His deep, throaty laugh filled the shower stall. "Just trying to help."

"You can help by letting me rinse off—handsy."

"Handsy?" Denver erupted into full-on gleeful chuckle as he took the handheld shower down, rinsed himself off, and then sprayed my backside.

"Give me that." I snapped the handheld from him and started rinsing my hard cock as he opened the shower door and left me to it. With more space, I finished sooner than if he'd been in there with me. My Alpha was immense and took up much of the shower space.

Toweling off needed to be quick.

Two minutes later, and we were jogging down the steps to Denver's truck. We held hands as he drove. Again, he left me to process. I'd had sex with someone I loved for the first time in my life. I picked at a loose thread on my pant leg. It was the first time I'd had sex since my last sex party. I'd been used by nine males that night—all of them human.

When in heat, my dad and uncle hadn't wanted to risk my getting pregnant by having bears breed me. Humans couldn't get me pregnant.

If I were with cub, they wanted it to be by one of them.

Fuck.

I held my face in my hand, crumpling forward, as fresh trails of wet poured down my cheeks. They'd tease me when I was in heat, telling me I reeked of Omega pussy. That I was useless and only good for being pumped full of cum and producing litter after litter of cubs.

Then they'd fuck the life out of me.

Ultimately, the fear of having a cub with one of them was what made me run.

I wouldn't have been able to protect it.

I leaned hard against the passenger door as Denver swerved and slammed on his brakes, skidding onto the edge of the dirt road to my cabin. It had been impossible to hide my despair.

"What's happening, Rory?" Both his hands enveloped the one he'd been holding. I knew if I looked at Denver, he would have concern etched into every pore on his face.

"Bad memories." I peered over at him, and my pulse quickened. Worse than etched. His expression was streaked with dark layers of agonizing despair. "Nothing to do with us. I was thinking about the last time I had sex. The last time I was bred."

I frowned as his face twisted. He didn't like the word *bred*.

I yanked my hand back and crossed my arms.

"That's what it was, Denver. They were breeding me. Male after male after male."

The sound of him breathing heavily filled the cab, but his expression softened. "You promised me you weren't going to try to scare me off anymore."

I closed my eyes and shook my head. "I wasn't trying to. I'm just panicking."

"About what?"

"About what happens if I go into heat." I turned in my seat to study every detail of his eyes.

"What do you mean *what happens*?"

There it is again.

Love.

"You said you don't want cubs."

Denver's brow dipped. "I said I didn't want cubs if it meant losing you." He set his hand on my thigh. "Whatever you want, Rory. Cubs ... no cubs. I'm not going anywhere."

I linked my fingers with his. "Sorry, my mind is a mess of emotions."

"Let's get you home." Denver pulled back onto the road, and within a few minutes, we reached the cabin. Denver had just shut off the engine and removed his keys from the ignition when the front door flew open, and Jesse emerged with Carter hobbling behind him.

I probably should've called them last night.

Jesse's face was contorted and crimson as he thundered down the steps and yanked open my passenger door. "I had to hear it from Harlan! Harlan! That the East Creekside wolf pack was called to Growlers ... to save you! And then you disappear like a fucking magic trick!"

"Jesse ...."

"And then I'm told, two outside bears ... who I am assuming were your dad and uncle, are dead in the center of Creekside!" Jesse pointed at Denver. "Murdered by your bear there!"

"Jesse ...."

"What!"

"I'm all right."

Jesse growled as he looked between Denver and me. "You mated with him."

Good nose.

"I did, and it's not open for discussion or dissection." I leaned toward Denver and rubbed my thumb across his lips before kissing them. I wanted to remember everything about them.

"Love you," he said.

I smiled at him. "Love you, too."

"You okay to get to work?"

"I'll figure it out."

I climbed from the truck and shut the door. Jesse stuck to me like tar paper as we mounted the steps to the porch. He nudged me. "We *are* going to talk about *that*."

"What *that*?" I knew what he was talking about.

"The part where you fell in love without telling us." Carter held the door open for us. The living room looked like they'd had a party in my absence. There were bottles and cans everywhere.

Jesse caught my look of concern.

"We were stress drinking," he said. "Figured you were at Denver's. Didn't know for sure."

"Jonas saw us leave together. You could have asked him."

Carter picked up a few cans and cradled them in his arms. "*You* could have called us."

"I know. I'm sorry. Things got intense last night."

"Your Alpha killed your dad and uncle," Carter said. "Intense is an understatement."

"When did you know you were in love with him?" Jesse returned to the first subject.

"I've known for a while. Made it official this morning." I looked down at my clothes. They had blood on them. Not sure whose. "Can you two give me a second to change for work?"

"You're going to work?" Carter lined up some bottles on the kitchen counter.

"Jonas shifted and tried to protect me from them. The least I can do is show up for work."

"You're made of tougher stuff than me," Carter said.

"Denver brings it out in me."

"Still not convinced," Jesse muttered. I watched him as he poured himself a vodka and orange juice. He didn't work today, but it was too early to be starting on the drinking. I was worried about him. Even though he was on methadone, he'd gone through vicious withdrawal. That's when he'd started drinking. Carter was of no help because he already had an alcohol problem.

Later.

I went to my room and picked out some clean clothes. With the money I was earning, I planned to buy more clothes and get a proper haircut. I wanted to look good for Denver *and* myself.

I lifted a pack of cigarettes off the dresser, looked at them, and tossed them in the trash. Not sure when it happened for sure, but even the thought of smoking one made me feel ill.

The walk through the woods to work was both calm *and* invigorating. I arrived at Growlers feeling good about the world. My life and my place in it felt secure.

Jonas' eyebrows rose when he saw me come in through the door.

"I was expecting you to call in sick."

"Nope." I smiled at him. "Denver and I are in love, and I'm feeling ready for anything. I've never felt as good as I do today."

"Well then ...." Jonas placed my apron on the counter. "Better get started." As I reached for the apron, Jonas put his hand on it. "You're glowing. It's nice to see that radiating off you."

"Thanks, Jonas."

He was right. I felt like I was glowing.

My dad and uncle were dead.

I was in love.

And I felt like I had found my place in the world.

I was happy.

I launched into my work and found myself chatting and laughing with the customers. I had Denver to thank for opening me up to the world around me.

I had Denver to thank for giving me my life back.

CHAPTER 16

DENVER

Saturday was my one day a week when I got to play. There was something about spending time with the town's youth that filled my soul—made me feel hopeful for the future.

The kids who came to the youth programs at the community center were awesome. We were playing a modified game of basketball with only three a side. It was mayhem, but it was a blast.

I had to make a point of not using my size to barrel through the other side's single defense player. I gave them a fair shot at stealing the ball, but once I was past them, dunking was my reward. At six-foot-seven, I didn't need to reach much to drop the ball through the net.

I glanced up, and there, leaning against the doorframe of the gymnasium, was Shaun, the youth coordinator. He'd moved to Creekside Valley around the same time that Rick and I did.

Shaun had been sitting in Maddox Black's living room, waiting, when we emerged from Maddox's office. Turns out Shaun was one of the four cougar shifters in town who came out. The wolf pack leader would know the actual count. Even I had caught a whiff of a few others.

I jogged over to him.

Shaun smiled at me and shifted his weight, accentuating the low-cut jeans he was wearing that exposed his midriff. "You're wearing them out. That's good."

His voice was an octave or more higher than most males, had a singsong, wispy quality, and he fluttered his hands around as he spoke. He was by far the most flamboyant male in town.

"Always here to help," I replied.

"Which is why I came to find *you*."

He stepped forward and placed his finger on my chest. It was an on-going game with him. Shaun flirted with me mercilessly even though I'd told him I wasn't interested in cougars.

I placed my hands on my hips. "What's up?"

"I'm playing musical chairs with the offices, and I need some desks moved around." He brushed his hand from my chest to my shoulder, then moved away. "Can you help?"

"Sure thing."

"Excellent."

I followed Shaun's swaying hips down the hall to the bank of offices. There were four in total: the community center manager, the adult activities coordinator, the bookkeeper, and Shaun.

"Darlene needs a bigger office to contain all the filing cabinets, books, and papers she's accumulated for the adult programs. I'm switching her with the bookkeeper."

"So, you'll need me to shift the filing cabinets, too."

Shaun placed his hand on his chest as if he were touching pearls. "You don't mind, do you?"

"No, of course not. Anything for you, sweetheart."

Shoot me. I could flirt right back. Shaun knew I wasn't serious. It was the banter we had fallen into over the years, even though I knew he wanted to jump my bones. But nothing beyond that.

Shaun wasn't a relationship cougar. He travelled to Metro City every weekend to hit the nightclubs and find someone to take him back to their place for a quick fuck.

His hand fluttered onto his cheek. "My stars, you will be the end of me."

I chuckled and stepped into Darlene's office. Thankfully, someone had put all her books and papers into boxes to be moved. It might be easier to empty the bookkeeper's office first.

I spent the next three hours shunting around the heavy and bulky contents of two offices. Shaun and the bookkeeper, Peter, helped me where they could by carrying boxes.

Using my muscles like that had me itching to let my bear out when we were done. When I got back to my office at the work site, I snuck off into the forest, shifted, and ran until I was tired.

It was late afternoon by the time I returned, and I was starving. I'd forgotten to pack a lunch today or pick anything up, so I called Growlers to place a delivery order.

"Growlers, how can I help you?"

My heart bloody well sang upon hearing Rory's voice.

"I need more kisses from you."

I could practically hear Rory smiling down the phone line. "I'm at work, Alpha."

I wished I could see the crimson blush on his face and the way he was probably biting his bottom lip. "I need to place a lunch order. Any chance you could bring it out to me?"

"I can ask." Long pause. "I'd have to borrow Jonas' car."

"He won't mind. Can you bring me a bear platter? I'll pay cash when you get here."

"I'll see what I can do. Love you." Then he hung up.

"Love you, too," I said to absolutely no one.

It had been a week since Rory's dad and uncle had come looking for him. He spoke to me less often about what he'd endured as a child. I hoped it was fading into the background. I knew it would never be gone. He still had nightmares. He still woke up crying out and clinging to me.

I walked his dreams every night, watching for the terror-filled, black hole to open in the forest as we ran and played in bear form there. Sometimes I caught Rory in time, sometimes I didn't.

I would be torn from my sleep when I failed, and I would do my best to comfort Rory by holding him. The first couple of nights, he had fought me, but that stopped. Now, he welcomed my embrace. Burrowed into it. Snuffled and sniffed my skin until he fell asleep again.

Rory hadn't gone home to sleep since we'd first made love. He'd spent every night this past week with me. Yesterday, he'd brought a few changes of clothes over with him.

It was like he'd moved in.

I didn't have a single argument against that.

Half an hour later, I heard tires crunching the gravel outside my office. I looked out the window and was thrilled to see it was Rory. He was carrying a large paper bag.

He'd never been to my office before, so I poked my head out into the grand front entry of the massive log structure that housed my office staff so he'd know where to go.

"Hey," he said after he stepped through the door and walked with haste toward me. He rose onto his toes and used one hand to steady my face as he pressed a perfect kiss to my lips.

"Mm ... I should have you deliver food to me more often."

Rory surveyed the entry. "Impressive. I guess it needs to be for the customers."

"Yeah, we need to show off our craftsmanship." I placed my hand on his lower back and guided him through the door into my office. He put the paper bag on my desk.

"I'd love to get a tour of everything you do here."

"Yeah?" My eyebrows peaked. I hadn't thought he'd be interested in my company. But then, of course, he would. We were in love. We had much to discover about one another.

"Can your lunch wait?" he asked.

"Absolutely." I led him out the door and across the yard to the first of our massive, covered work areas, where we assembled the build. We would then number and label every piece for reassembly on the customer's property, where the home would stand for centuries to come.

Rory wandered around the home we were working on, eyes scanning, mouth open, arms hanging at his sides. Not crossed. Not with his hands stuffed in his pockets like he usually did.

He was enthralled.

He pointed at one of the harnessed workers straddling a log and guiding another log into place. "What do you have to do to get a job like that?"

"We train them on the job. They're shadowed for a few months until they get the hang of it." I stroked my chin, not sure where he was going with this. "Why do you ask?"

He turned to face me, and I'd never seen such wonder in his eyes.

"I'd love to try it," he said.

Shocked. More than I should be. Rory was the right build to be up there placing logs, but his experience was in tinkering with mechanical stuff.

"You're serious?" I caught up with him as he continued to circle the build. He ran his hand along one of the logs. The way he caressed the logs warmed my heart.

"You can feel it, can't you?" I asked.

"It's like they're still alive. Placing them together in a magnificent structure is like paying them homage." He stopped and looked up at one of the workers. "I'm serious. I want to do that."

My heart pattered hard, loud in my ears. Being able to see Rory every day and work with him would bring us closer than I ever could have imagined our lives might turn out to be.

"You're hired."

Rory spun around to face me. "Really?"

"Yeah, you're lean, but you're a bear, so you're stronger than the humans up there."

He rushed to me and wrapped his arms around my waist. I didn't care if anyone saw us. They'd soon find out what Rory meant to me, especially if he was working here.

"When can I start?"

"How about Monday?"

I got a wide, toothy grin out of Rory. "I'll break the news to Jonas when I get back to work. I hope he's not upset that I'm ditching him."

I stroked Rory's cheek. "He'll be more than fine with it. He wants you to be happy."

Rory turned back to the build. "This is going to make me *very* happy."

"Happier than when you're kissing me?"

Rory laughed, then turned and ran into an embrace I had waiting for him.

"Never."

And then he kissed me. Right there in front of everyone. There were a few cat calls and whistles. I knew my team of workers would support me and treat Rory with respect.

I couldn't wait to fold Rory into our work family.

And hopefully, my home family.

Two weeks later, and I still hadn't worked up the courage to ask Rory to make our relationship permanent. To announce to the world that we were forever mates.

We'd been working together, and it had been incredible, seeing him every day. He had taken to the job like he was always meant to do it. And the glow in his eyes—priceless.

I sat at the kitchen dining table watching Rory. The bear would honestly eat anything, and it was starting to show, especially in his belly. I loved how he now had a thin layer of fat on him.

I pressed my hand to my jeans' pocket. It was still there—always there. The small box containing what I had bought the night I killed Rory's dad and uncle.

It was wearing a hole in my pants.

"Can we go sit on the porch when we're done? The stars are bright tonight."

"Sure." Rory scraped every crumb and remnant of sauce off his plate into his mouth.

"Meet you out there?" I rose and took my dishes to the dishwasher. Rory still had his mountainous dessert to get through. I'd given the one he set in front of me a hard pass.

I took a seat in one of the porch chairs and stared out into the sky. Someone had brought Rory all the way from Metro City to me. He'd changed where I saw my life going.

I felt the box in my pocket again.

I whipped my hand away from it when Rory emerged from the house. I patted my lap, and he sat on it and leaned back against my shoulder. I wrapped my arms around him.

"It *is* nice out tonight," he said. "A bit chilly, but nice."

I nuzzled the side of his neck, enjoying the aroma of him.

The time is now.

I reached into my pocket and pried the box from the creases of my jeans. I wasn't sure what to do with it, so I held it awkwardly in front of Rory.

Rory touched it. "What's this?"

"It's me asking you something." I kissed his ear. "Marry me."

There it was out.

I'd asked the love of my life to marry me.

I waited for his answer.

CHAPTER 17

RORY

It had been over three weeks since we first mated, and I was sure I knew what was going on. Four days ago, I'd woken up with the urge to run to the toilet and throw up.

I'd rested my cheek on the porcelain and drooled into the water instead.

I swallowed, Denver's words settling deep in my heart.

Marry me.

I took the small box from his hand and opened the lid as if seeing the ring would decide whether I wanted to marry him or not. I stroked it with my finger.

I'd made my decision as soon as he spoke the words to me. I lifted the ring and sent it on its monumental journey down my finger. Denver chuckled and kissed my cheek.

I still hadn't spoken.

I sat up straight so I could turn to face him. "Yes, and I need to tell you something."

Denver beamed at me. I could've kissed his smile right off his face.

"Anything," he said.

I took a deep breath. *Here goes nothing.* "I think I'm pregnant."

His expression fell for a split second, then it came back brighter than moments before when I told him I would marry him. His hand was on my stomach before I could blink.

"You're sure?" He looked from my belly into my eyes.

"Surely, you've noticed how much rounder I'm getting."

"I thought I was feeding you too much."

I laughed. "Probably part of the issue. But yes ... I'm pretty sure. I feel ... odd." I placed my hand on his, which was cupping my stomach. "We'll know for sure in another month or so."

"What about a pregnancy test?"

I shook my head. "No. I don't like those." My dad had been particularly eager for me to get pregnant by him or my uncle. I hated the sight of pregnancy tests. He would make me carry the used ones in my teeth for hours to remind me how useless I was when the test came back negative.

Denver backed off the idea. Didn't ask me why I didn't like them. He knew I would talk when I wanted to. He would never push me to share when something didn't make sense to him.

My Alpha wrapped his arms around me, hugged me tightly, and kissed my head.

"I've never been more thrilled," he said. "Our engagement and a cub ... in one day."

I relaxed against him. "I love you."

"My sweet Omega, you and this little cub are my life."

I stroked his cheek.

A life I share with you.

"When do you want to get married?" I asked.

"Today, if I could."

I smiled against his neck. "We might need more time than that."

"I'll talk to Maddox. He's the nuptial officiant in Creekside."

I rolled my eyes and laughed. "Of course, he is."

"You're in wolf pack country." He tugged me to him. "Better get used to it."

"I'm getting there."

"So ... are you officially moving in, or are we going to wait until we're married?"

I gently shoved him. "What do you think, Alpha? It'll take me exactly two minutes to gather up everything else I own and head over here with it. Why would we wait?"

"I can't think of a single reason."

"Good."

I held up my hand and examined the engagement ring from all sides. It was a simple silver band with a small diamond set in it. It was perfect. Understated with a small amount of bling.

Denver clung to me, rose to his feet, and lifted me. I wrapped my arms around his neck and hung on as he took me inside the house and upstairs to the bedroom.

He laid me on the bed and started with my shirt, removing it with such care. Next, he shimmied my pants and underwear off. Without undressing, Denver climbed onto the bed. He went straight for my stomach, caressing it, then kissed it, humming on my skin.

"Hello, little cub," he said against my belly.

I grinned and ran my hand through his hair. He was going to make an exceptional sire. A few more kisses, and Denver trailed his lips to my chest. I'd thought it was me getting fat, but near the end of the past week, my pecs had an added softness, and my nipples had become puffy.

Denver needed room, so I opened my legs so he could lie between them. His arms on either side of my ribcage, he brushed his thumbs over what had once been hard nubs.

"Mm ... I was wondering what was going on here," he said. He shifted closer and took one into his mouth. I felt a pull from behind it as he sucked gently.

He switched to the other nipple. The same pulling sensation had me moaning and squirming, my ass digging into the mattress. I thrust my hips up, grinding against Denver's body.

Denver kissed the center of my chest. "My Omega."

I tousled his hair. "Are you going to get rid of your clothes?"

"Not yet." He moved down my body, set his lips on my skin from my breastbone to the dark, curly hair above my cock. I closed my eyes as he sucked my soft dick into his mouth.

So good.

Bobbing, suction, and using his tongue, he soon had me hard. I breathed through the slight patter of anxiety. Then it was gone, and it was just Denver and me again.

He used his hand to cup and caress my balls as he rode my cock with his mouth. A coil of desperation curled in my gut. I was so close. I imagined him filling me with his beautiful cum.

My entire body felt overstimulated ... alive.

Slivers of ecstasy crept under my skin.

My dick pulsed, so tight.

I whimpered, then let out the most fulfilled roar of my life, and flooded Denver's throat. He loved drinking me down. It had taken me a while to get comfortable with him bringing me to climax with his mouth. I'd had so many bad memories to work through.

I'd been going to therapy for the past two weeks. Sometimes it helped, and on some days, I came away feeling raw, like a stripped, exposed wire.

On those days, I would run home and straight into Denver's arms. He was my haven—the person who knew me better than anyone.

We'd had many frank conversations. I'd walked him through *almost everything* that had ever happened to me. Some things would hurt him too much.

I had no intention of traumatizing him.

But guided by my therapist, I'd revealed the information that he should know. Things that pertained to my perspective on the world. As for touch, I still couldn't stand being touched by others. Denver was the only one who could be that close to me.

I snuggled against Denver's chest when he came up the bed to lie beside me. He smelled of cedar from being at work. I loved coming home with the scent of the logs on me.

I'd taken to the new job like it was in my blood. Working with trees filled a need in me that I liked to trace back to my being a bear. Forests existed and thrived within me.

I couldn't thank Carter enough for pushing Jesse and me to follow his dream.

The hair on Denver's chest was golden from the amber-colored light beside the bed. I pushed my fingers through it. Carter and Jesse were happy for me.

Jesse still didn't trust Denver, but then he rarely trusted anyone. He was drawn to breaking his view of the world by drowning himself in alcohol. I was surprised he hadn't lost his job.

Carter was thriving most days. He'd recently revealed to us that he was seeking treatment for depression. Not that I hadn't noticed when he went dark. Carter was such a positive person. Having him sink into depression was worrying. I suspected his past pulled him down into it.

I fell asleep in Denver's arms.

He met me there ... in my dreams.

He always met me there. We had such magical times together in the fantasy forest we'd built for ourselves. Sometimes a pinpoint of black would appear. Most nights, it didn't succeed in pulling me into it. Other nights, it couldn't be helped. Even Denver couldn't keep me from it.

He was always there when I woke.

The following eight months passed quickly. We'd married a month after Denver asked me, and I'd left work during my seventh month of pregnancy, too sore and big to do the job.

I missed it as much as if someone had stopped me from breathing. We often went there in my dreams to drink in the scent and feel of the logs. They brought me peace.

My due date had come and gone, and I was desperate to see my cub. I was huge and uncomfortable the day every muscle in my uterus felt as if it was trying to kill me.

I found Denver in the kitchen doing dishes and grabbed his arm in a vice grip.

"It's time."

"Um ... okay." He frantically dried his hands. "Let's get outside."

"Hardly going to shift in the house."

Fuck.

I bent over, clutching my stomach. "Help me get out there."

Denver took my arm and guided me to the edge of the forest. Wolves could give birth to their pups in human form—no such luck as a bear. Our cubs were too big.

Increasing my pain, I stripped and shifted alongside Denver, who did the same.

I padded as quickly as I could, headed for the den we'd made. The cool earth surrounded me as I descended into it. Denver would wait outside until our cub made its appearance.

I lay down on my side and breathed through every contraction. One final push and our cub was out. I scrambled to the other side of the den to check on it. It wasn't breathing. My instincts kicked in, and I started licking it. On one of my passes, I discovered it was a female.

I snorted when she took her first breath, then picked her up and brought her back to where I'd been lying. I plopped her down next to one of my nipples and called for my Alpha.

"Denver."

He grunted as he entered the den, blocking the light, then came to my side and nudged our cub, inhaling her scent to imprint it on his mind.

He nudged my snout next. I snuck my tongue out and licked the corner of his mouth. It wasn't typical bear behavior for him to be here with me, but we did things differently.

Our love was more wolflike than bear.

Nothing could separate us.

I sniffed our cub's little head. *"She looks like a Cleo."*

"She certainly does."

With that decided, I closed my eyes. I was exhausted. I felt movement as Denver used his snout to encourage Cleo to feed. She latched on, and a rush of euphoria overcame me.

Then I felt myself sinking into the soil.

So tired.

My life had taken a turn I never thought I'd be able to achieve. A mate and cub I loved was more than I'd been conditioned to expect.

"Love you, Omega."

"Mm ... love you, too."

Then I fell asleep and dreamed of our life together. Denver let me enjoy it on my own for a few minutes. Then he appeared, and he saw how I expected our lives to unfold.

More cubs.

Grand cubs.

A life of bliss.

Love ... so much love.

UNREDEEMABLE

CREEKSIDE VALLEY – BOOK 2

He never thought he deserved forgiveness. He certainly never expected love.

Carter has been running from the wreckage of his past for years. A bear shifter haunted by a drunken car crash that claimed the lives of his brother, cousin, and stepsister-girlfriend, he's learned to survive by disappearing—into the shadows, into the streets of Metro City, and into the arms of strangers. With a shattered body and scarred face, he's convinced himself he's unredeemable. He's a killer, and killers don't deserve happy endings.

But when he escapes from the city with his two best friends and lands in the quiet town of Creekside, everything begins to change. There, he meets Shaun—a bold, unapologetically flamboyant cougar shifter who sees Carter's pain... and sees through it.

Carter doesn't know if he's ready for love, or if he even deserves it. But Shaun isn't the type to let fear win. As Carter confronts his past, heals old wounds, and reclaims parts of himself he thought were lost forever, he discovers that sometimes, the fiercest kind of love is the one that finds you when you're broken.

Raw, tender, and ultimately hopeful, *Unredeemable* is a shifter romance about redemption, the power of love, and the courage to heal and find peace.

Buy or Read Now!

ABOUT THE AUTHOR

J T Fader is the fantasy and paranormal pen name of queer, bigender author Leigh Jarrett (she/he). Writing MM+ romance with a speculative twist, JT Fader explores magical worlds, supernatural beings, and otherworldly love stories filled with emotion, grit, and passion.

Their work blends the fantastical with deep character connection, featuring queer protagonists on transformative journeys.

Based on Vancouver Island, JT Fader brings the same heart and authenticity found in Leigh Jarrett's contemporary work to realms of magic, myth, and epic fantasy.

To check out more of JT Fader's titles, go to their website